WITCH THIS WAY

A HOLIDAY HILLS WITCH COZY MYSTERY

CAROLYN RIDDER ASPENSON

Severn River
PUBLISHING

WITCH THIS WAY

Severn River Publishing
www.SevernRiverPublishing.com

This is a work of fiction. Names, characters, businesses, places, events and incidents are either the products of the author's imagination or used in a fictitious manner. Any resemblance to actual persons, living or dead, or actual events is purely coincidental.

ISBN: 978-1-64875-015-1 (Paperback)

Join Carolyn's Newsletter List at

CarolynRidderAspenson.com

You'll receive a free novella as a thank you!

To Jack
For always believing in me

CHAPTER 1

*B*eing a witch is complicated. A witch must lie, cheat, and sometimes even steal—though that's rare–to protect their secret. See, witches aren't allowed to tell humans about their magic. It goes against the code of ethics.

I haven't actually seen the code of ethics, but I hear going against it comes with some seriously steep consequences, like being banished from the world or stripped of power. I like being part of the world, and since my powers are relatively new, I'd prefer to keep them and see what they can do. Powers I'd never asked for, by the way, but for the most part have learned to enjoy.

My mother Addie Odell was a witch, and from everything I've learned, I come from a family of powerful witches and warlocks. I've also discovered they were quite emotional and made rash decisions. At least I know where I get that from. When my mom died, the binding spell she'd placed on me died with her. Out of nowhere, I'd scratch my nose—which happens often during allergy season—and stuff happened. Things flew across rooms, people tripped, and one time a crotchety old man who needed an attitude adjustment lost his pants. They only fell to the ground, they didn't disappear, but still, I felt pretty bad about that. It took some time, but I've figured out how to manage things a lot better.

I learned my mother's best friend Bessie, the woman I consider family, is also a witch. She owns The Enchanted, an adorable book and coffee shop in the heart of Holiday Hills. If you need a book, Bessie has it. If you need a cup of coffee with a pinch of magic, she's got that too. Bessie's been by my side since I discovered my witchy ways, and I don't know what I'd do without her.

I can be my true self around Bessie, but being a witch means hiding your powers from your human best friend, who thankfully can't see when something magical happens. Humans see something different, which takes some getting used to when I'm chatting with my bestie and a shapeshifting wolf stops by to say hey.

Stella is the yin to my yang. She's high-maintenance, smart, and gorgeous, and has this way with people that makes me wish I were her. If I didn't love her so much, I'd probably hate her, mostly because she's petite and I have to duck to get through most doors. At least I don't have to duck at The Enchanted. Bessie made the door high enough for me when I hit my head on it a few years back.

As I sat in my makeshift office—a table to the side of Bessie's counter at The Enchanted—and worked on my latest novel, I thought about how much my life had changed in the past year. I lost my mom and a man I considered a friend, but I'd gained a sort-of boyfriend, a whole lot of powers, and another *USA Today* best-seller tag for an author I'd grown to despise.

Authors are such divas.

My latest paranormal cozy mystery novel, *There's a Whole Lotta Witching Going On*, was shaping up nicely so far. I still had a way to go, but I was pleased with what I'd already written. But if the writer who took all the credit didn't get off my back, I'd probably turn her into a toad. Trust me, she deserved it. Writing a best seller takes time, and she'd just have to put up and shut up if she wasn't going to do the actual work.

Bessie poured me a cup of tea. It was cold outside, and the hot liquid warmed me from the inside. I shivered as the brew seeped into my veins. "That's good stuff."

"It ought to be. I worked hard on it." She sat across from me and peeked at my pile of notes. "This one's tough, huh?"

"It's not that. It's just…I don't know how to explain it. It's giving me a little déjà vu kind of feeling."

"How so?"

"Esmerelda meets a guy, and he doesn't know she's a witch."

Her eyes widened. "Oh, my."

"They always say write what you know."

"Who are *they*?"

I shrugged. "Apparently, that's a secret."

She smiled. "I'm sure you've got this, sugar."

"I appreciate that. At least I can write out my issues and frustrations through my characters."

"I'm sure that's helpful. How does your witch save the world in this one?"

"She's not saving the world, just her own neck of the woods. And at the moment, it's an evil warlock with a love for arson."

Her eyes widened. "That doesn't sound all that cozy."

I shrugged. "You know how it works. Things happen off the page, no cats are killed, happy ending for all except the bad guy."

My Burmese cat Cooper, who doubled as my familiar, lifted his head from a bowl of Chicken of the Sea. "Dude. Killing cats is never cool."

I pointed my finger at him. "I know that."

Bessie smiled at Cooper, then turned back to me. "You've got this."

"I do have it, it's just weird writing about me and Gabe, sort of."

She smiled. "Maybe you should push your fictional couple into a stronger relationship and see what happens between you and our police chief?"

My stomach flipped. "I like how it's going at the moment. It's new and fun and exciting, and I don't get mad if he chooses to hang with the boys instead of with me."

"Gabe doesn't strike me as the type to hang with the boys."

"He's not, but if he were, I wouldn't be mad. It's casual. I like it that way."

She winked at me. "Hmm hmm."

"What?"

She stood and sauntered back to the counter. "I thought you had a backbone. Guess I was wrong."

"Ouch."

Ryland Augustus, a man who'd moved to Holiday Hills three months ago, walked into The Enchanted. He smiled at us and moved toward the empty leather chairs near the display window. I stiffened as he went to sit. When his body molded into the old, softened leather chair once saved for someone I'd tried to forget, he shook and all but jumped out of it.

He caught us staring at him and shrugged. "Not as comfy as I thought." His voice was deep, reminding me of the mall Santa my mother took me to when I was six. He had such a powerful, low voice, I wanted to repent for all my naughtiness over the last year just to get a gift.

"You're not the first to say that," Bessie said. "What can I get you this morning, Ryland?"

"I'd love a black coffee. You know me. Nothing special."

She smiled and muttered, "You're special to all of us," under her breath.

I shook my head. Ryland was my age, and yes, he was very attractive. Dark, shaggy hair and a chiseled face like a Greek God. His blue eyes and lashes-to-die-for kept all the women in town drooling, but he didn't seem all that interested. He'd come for a job, he told us. Would be in town a few months until he finished, and then he'd head back to New York.

I couldn't put my finger on it, but something about Ryland made the hairs on the back of my neck rise every time I saw him. He would ask me questions about myself, but when I asked him something, he became a politician who didn't want to answer. He'd either change the subject or answer in a way that didn't actually tell me anything.

He leaned against the counter and nodded at me. "You're a writer, correct?"

"Yup. Working on the next book in a series as we speak."

He stepped closer and tried to eye my screen. I shifted my arm in front of it. I didn't want strangers knowing what I wrote.

"What's it about?"

I waved him off. "Oh, it's nothing, really."

Bessie handed him a drink. "Don't let her fool you. Abby is an international bestselling author. She is very famous."

I shook my head. "No, I'm not. I promise."

"Excuse me," Bessie said, smiling. "Her books are famous, but she doesn't take any credit for them."

"What kind of books do you write?"

I blushed. "I'd, uh, I'd rather not say."

"Oh, don't be silly. She writes paranormal cozy mysteries about witches and shapeshifters. She's very good, too."

He raised an eyebrow, and I thought he might bust out laughing. "Shapeshifters?"

"You know, things that turn into other things." I bit my bottom lip. "It's a big genre. Women and even some men love these kinds of books, but I have a feeling you'd be bored. Who's your favorite author?"

"I'm a Stephen King fan."

I nodded. "Yeah, my books are a little too G-rated for you, then."

"Maybe not. What's the storyline? Does the witch fight evil?"

I shrugged. "In a friendly, no-one-dies-on-the-page kind of way, yeah."

"No one dies on the page?"

"G-rated, remember?"

He smiled, and I thought his teeth sparkled.

As attractive as he was, my heart was already taken, and I wasn't all that interested in anything temporary.

Stella stormed through the door. "If this flipping author doesn't get her gosh darn butt in gear I'm going to lose—" She shut up the minute she saw Ryland. "Oh, hey," she said, batting her eyelashes.

Bessie glanced at me with a raised brow. I smirked.

If Ryland noticed Stella's embarrassment, he pretended not to notice. "Hey, Stella, how are you?"

"I'm good." She scooted to the counter, her face as red as the tomato I'd sliced for my salad last night.

It took everything I had not to laugh. I didn't know for sure, but I suspected Ryland wasn't a magical, though he'd definitely worked his magic on most of the women in town.

Stella picked a muffin off the counter and slunk to my table.

"I'm serious," she whispered. "If she doesn't take my professional advice, I'm going to lose it." She tossed her backpack onto my table and plopped into the seat warmed by Bessie, then tossed her head back and whined, "I cannot stand this woman!"

While Stella and I don't share a magical lifestyle, we do share a love for fiction. She's a fiction editor, one without a whole lot of patience, something an editor truly needs when dealing with creative people. She's the best I've met, and I've run things by her several times, but I don't use her for my books. Even if my publisher didn't provide an editor, I wouldn't. Sometimes it's best to keep the personal part of life out of the professional one. "What's the problem now?"

"She doesn't know how to split scenes. They all just run together like one big dragged out—" She threw her hands over her head and waved them around. "Mess. I made some suggestions for changes and she literally called me crying." She shook her head. "Crying? What the hecking heck is that!"

The side of my mouth threatened to curve upward. I did my best to stop it because I didn't want to make light of her frustration. Stella has a truckdriver's mouth, which she's worked hard to curb. She used to just say things like *blankety-blank* and *dog poop*, but she's upped her swearing game. It was hard to take her seriously when she fake swore.

"Stop it."

I tilted my head. "What?"

"I know you're trying not to laugh at me." She pivoted toward Bessie, who quickly gave her a view of her back. "You too!"

We all laughed.

Ryland smiled at us as he returned a newspaper to the counter. "Nice to see you, ladies. Have a nice day."

"Going so soon?" Bessie asked. "I've got a quiche in the oven in back. I could get you a piece to go for lunch? Just take a minute."

Bessie's bookstore wasn't an official café, but over the years, her initial menu of coffees and teas expanded to cookies, light sandwiches, and the occasional soup or quiche. Last week she added some salads to her unofficial menu, and the Caesar became my favorite.

"I'm good, but thanks. I'm sure I'll see you soon, though."

Stella ogled him as he walked out, a slight moan slipping from her lips. "He's so yummy."

I ignored her. "You know you can't force a writer to change their story. You can only help to improve it."

She sighed. "I know, but you know I'm a control freak, so what's a girl to do?"

"Get counseling?"

She rolled her eyes. "As if." She unzipped her backpack and pulled out her laptop. "How's Esmerelda doing these days?"

"She's sort of working for the MBI now and it's interfering with her new relationship."

"MBI?"

"Magical Bureau of Investigations. Duh."

"Oh, sorry. I should have known. I hear the MBI is big here in Holiday Hills."

If she only knew.

"Speaking of relationships…"

I held out my hand. "Don't go there."

She palmed her chest. "Me? Never."

"They're going to have lunch together this afternoon," Bessie said. Her eyes disappeared as she gave me a puffy-cheeked smile.

"OMG! Seriously?"

"What are you, twelve?"

"Can't a bestie be happy for her friend?"

"You're not happy. You're shocked. There's a difference."

"Of course I'm happy. I mean, yeah, I'm shocked, but I'm happy. You're like, you know, almost having a real relationship. It's about time."

I pushed my laptop aside. I wasn't getting anything done anyway. "I know, and that kind of freaks me out. I am excited, sure, but I'm really nervous."

"Why? You've already been out with him. What's the difference?"

Because I didn't want to toss his gun across the room, and lately, my powers had been a bit wonky. Plus, things felt different between us. "I don't know. It's like we're dipping our toes into the pond of coupledom but can't quite stick the rest of our foot in."

She stared at me.

"What?"

"Sometimes I feel like you're hiding something from me."

Um. "What do you mean?"

"Your true feelings, maybe? You know you can tell me

anything, right?" She leaned toward me, and I knew the concern in her eyes was real. "I'm starting to worry about you."

I was officially the worst BFF ever. "I'm sorry I've made you feel that way. I'm not hiding anything from you. I'm still trying to figure out what I feel, you know what I mean?"

She smiled. "I know, and I get it. Just know I'm here for you."

"I know, and ditto."

Truth is, I am hiding things from Stella. A lot of things, as is most of town. For the past several months, since finding out about my witchy ways, I've kept Stella at arm's length. It's hard juggling the human and magical worlds. When I feel over-whelmed, I retreat inward, and lately, I've been far too deep inside my own head. I feel awful for that, for how it's impacted her, but I don't know what to do about it.

Stella stayed a few hours and worked through her client's manuscript while Esmerelda and I continued our adventure. I focused on my fictional witch's new job as an investigator with the MBI, and gave her an assignment that put her in jeopardy both physically and emotionally. Light drama and intensity are key to cozy mysteries, and Esmerelda's stories include both. She needs to grow, but I'm not sure yet how she will. That usually happens naturally as the story flows, but sometimes I need to push her a little more than others. Funny, I found when I did that, I needed to do it for myself too.

Esmerelda and I had a lot in common lately.

Esmerelda walked into the MBI office, her shoulders back, her head held high. I can do this, she told herself. I know I can. The MBI needed a strong witch, and Esmerelda was up to the task. For the most part anyway. Magically, she wasn't worried, but emotionally, she wasn't so sure. Could she help the investigators solve their hardest cases? Did she have what it took? If only she had the answers.

Esmerelda threw her purse onto the chair in her new office. Jake Manning, the local police chief, sauntered over, his big dark eyes penetrating the deepest part of her soul. Her heart skipped a beat and she couldn't breathe. Get it together, Es, he's just a man. You've got this.

Gabe Ryder walked into the bookstore. When he noticed me, his dark brown eyes burrowed into me with such powerful intensity, I squirmed. Oh, là là. The man did things to my soul.

It was alarming.

It had been almost a year since we began this back-and-forth tug of romantic war, and I couldn't tell if we were any closer to something committed than the day it all started. Our age differ-ence—one I chose to ignore—played a factor in things for him, as did his widower status. I think being romantically involved with someone scared him. Maybe he thought it was wrong because he still loved his wife? I didn't know, and it was best not to think about it. Even though I did, a lot.

His smile brightened the room. "How's the book coming along?"

"So far, so good."

Cooper climbed onto the back of my chair. He wasn't exactly Gabe's biggest fan, but cats weren't like dogs. Dogs looked for the good in people, while cats, especially Cooper, looked for food. Gabe never brought him a can of tuna, therefore Gabe was a horrible person.

He rubbed the side of his furry face into my neck. "I can feel the blood pumping through your carotid artery. Geez. Chill out."

I plucked him from my shoulder and tossed him to the tile floor. "Good boy," I lied.

Gabe eyed the cat, and Cooper hissed at him as he walked away. "That cat doesn't like me."

"Bring him a can of tuna, and he'll come around."

An awkward silence filled the air.

"Mr. Charming loves you, though." I smiled hesitantly because I wasn't quite sure that was the truth.

Gabe turned toward the back of the book shop, staring down the main aisle. "Where is the bird?"

"I think he's having breakfast in the back. Bess likes to leave him fresh berries in the morning."

"Not spoiled, is he?"

"Not at all."

"We still on for later today?"

I squirmed in my seat. "Uh, yeah. Of course. Noon sound good?"

"Can we make it one? I've got an eleven o'clock meeting, and they always run late."

"Perfect."

"Eddie's work for you?"

Eddie's is a small café on the outskirts of town, away from the hustle and bustle of our small magical city. "Sure."

A smile stretched across his handsome face. "Great. Gives us some privacy."

My heart raced, and I thought I'd have to stick my head between my knees to breathe again. "I'll be there."

He smiled again, and Bessie handed him his coffee to go.

I melted into a puddle of witchy goo as he strutted out the door.

About this afternoon is how Gabe's text appeared on my iPhone. I waited for the dots to disappear as he typed the next text that would say he needed to reschedule.

Something's come up. Need to reschedule.

No problem, I responded.

No dots. I wanted to toss my phone across the bookstore. I glanced at Bessie, but she wasn't paying attention, thank God. I kept at Esmerelda's story, refusing to let Gabe's blow-off get me down. I was on a deadline, after all. And besides, who was I to think I was more important than a city full of people? Gabe's job required his full attention, and the safety of his residents was more important than a lunch date.

Or so I told myself. I got back to work.

I crept into the small room at the back of the store. I knew the warlock was back there. I just wasn't sure how I'd handle him. He's the one, I thought. I could feel it in my bones.

Esmerelda was hunting a magical arsonist setting fires to important businesses in town. She knew the suspect had a reason, and she knew once the authorities figured out that reason they could determine his or her next move. I knew nothing about arson, so Google and I had become good friends. It's amazing what you can find on the internet.

My concentration went out the window with the sound of sirens blaring past The Enchanted. I watched the backs of two fire trucks and an ambulance leave dust on the street behind them. Three people in the store jumped to their feet and rushed to the window.

"What's going on?" Bessie hollered from the back.

"You see that smoke?"

Edison McRae opened the door and stepped onto the sidewalk. "Oh, Goddess. There's a fire. Look at that smoke."

I rushed to the door, practically shoving the old witch aside. "Whoa." Smoke filtered from Dr. Hetty's building down the street. I checked my watch. "It's after one. Doc's back from lunch." I took off in a run toward the sweet old witch doctor's small office. Doc had been my physician for years, and if he was in trouble, I should help.

Cooper and Mr. Charming followed me. I scooped my cat into my arms just in time for a red SUV to zip past. I might have hollered something unladylike at it as it sped by, then set Cooper down across the street and bolted again.

"Abby, hold up. I've got legs the size of a mouse," Cooper hollered.

He wasn't kidding. Those things were little nubs covered in soft brown fur.

"Get a move on, get a move on," Mr. Charming chirped.

Sometimes Mr. Charming was a wise guy. But it wasn't a time for jokes, which I quickly remembered when the scent of fire filled my nose and the black cloud rising in the sky threatened to turn it to midnight's darkness before ten a.m.

I stood outside my doctor's office, my jaw hanging open in pure shock. In seconds flat, fire had engulfed the small building. Two firemen rushed inside, and returned seconds later with Doc and his lifelong nurse, Ophelia.

Bad things didn't happen in the quaint town named Holiday Hills. Why not? Because magic lived here, and bad things weren't allowed to happen. Werewolves, shapeshifters, witches, and warlocks lived together in harmony, just like Michael Jackson and Paul McCartney. It was an unwritten law. A sometimes-broken unwritten law, but as far as I knew, we'd done a pretty good job of abiding by it. Sure, we'd had our problems, but for the most part, our little magical corner of the world was an anomaly.

The smoke burned my eyes. The fire department kept everyone several feet back from the building, but even though the gawkers were safe from the flames, the smoke filled our lungs, sending us into coughing fits.

A fireman spoke through a bullhorn. "I need everyone to step back, please."

A few people listened while others ignored the order. I was one of the latter, watching as he examined the small crowd gathering on the street. Two cars tried to pass, but people wouldn't move. He directed one of the fire trucks to the right, blocking the street completely and preventing onlookers from getting too close. A third Holiday Hills police officer parked his cruiser perpendicular to the fire truck, creating an even larger cushion from the heat and smoke. He blew his whistle and motioned the crowd to step back. When they didn't listen, he blew the whistle over and over until they did.

I took a few steps back, but kept as close to the front of the growing crowd as possible.

Bessie showed up behind me and gripped my shoulder. "Oh dear. We should do something, don't you think?"

I could barely hear her over the officer's incessant whistle blowing. "Like what?"

"Stop the fire, that's what!" She pushed me to the side and flung her arm toward the burning building. Flames shot out from the second-story windows as Doc's sign detached itself on one side, then the other, before finally falling to the sidewalk with a loud boom. I jerked back, fearing the flames would fly toward us, and wrapped my arms around Bessie to keep her safe.

She shook me away and flung her arms toward the burning building again, waving them in half circles as if she were scooping water from a lake and splashing it on the building.

It worked. The fire slowed to an ember-filled fizzle and then died.

The crowd dispersed, leaving only the firemen, Doc, his nurse Ophelia, Bessie, Gabe, and me standing there in awe.

"My files," Doc cried. "My patient files! They're gone. Everything I've ever diagnosed, thought, felt, or presumed about my patients, gone. Burned to ash." He held his head in his hands and cried while Ophelia patted him on the back.

I leaned toward Bessie and whispered, "Can he get those back?"

She tipped her head toward mine and sighed. "He can't do it himself. Personal gain."

I chewed on my bottom lip. "But it's not really. His patients need him, and to do a good job, he needs their records." Why hadn't he gone digital like the rest of the world?

"There's a fine line between helping others and helping yourself, Abby. Most magicals don't cross it. But you're right. He needs those files for more than personal gain." She tapped her finger to her chin. "I think we can help. As long as we don't bring back our own personal records, it should be fine for us to return the others."

I smiled. "You can bring mine, and I'll bring yours."

"That right there is what you call a magical loophole, sweetie."

I danced on the tips of my toes. "So, what're we waiting for?"

She hitched her head and said, "Nothing. Let's go."

We dragged poor Doc back to The Enchanted and told him our idea. He cried, then we cried, and then we all looked like blubbering idiots to the store's customers, but we didn't care. It felt good to do something so important.

How the human world deciphered the magic we hid from them never ceased to amaze me. Stella and Gabe saw that fire. They knew it destroyed the building and everything in it. But what they didn't know was whether Doc had his files digitally saved. He hadn't, but we changed that.

Thanks to a little nose bump and hand wave.

∽

E*smerelda followed the man into the dark alley, her hands shaking as beads of sweat pooled into drops streaming from her forehead. Everything in her magical soul told her he was the one. She knew she shouldn't follow him alone. She needed backup, but there was no time to make that call. Think fast, she told herself. Don't let him catch on. Fool him. Let him think you're naïve, that you don't know who he truly is.*

I slammed my forefinger on the delete key and started over. Essie, as I'd nicknamed her, was being a pain in the rear today, and wouldn't do what I told her. Trust me, when an author can't control her characters, it's never a good thing.

She tripped over a brick in the alley and fell to her knees. She stayed there, staring at the man ahead of her, hoping he hadn't heard, worried she'd just given her stalking game away. What was she thinking? She wasn't brave enough for this.

Esmerelda's confidence sank. Don't follow the man, she thought. It won't do you any good. He's dangerous, and you're not powerful enough to handle him.

Who was she kidding? She'd follow him. She knew what she was capable of, and she had to believe a simple human was no match for a witch. She stood, brushed the gravel from her pants, and took two steps forward. The alley was dark, and her eyes struggled to adjust. She stepped on a torn cardboard box, which rubbed against the gravel. She froze, holding her breath and praying to all things magical the man didn't hear.

He stopped and twisted his body toward her, and she ducked. The red of his eyes bore through the brick building behind her, leaving a small hole just a foot above her.

Dear Goblins, what is he? she thought.

He wasn't human. That much she knew.

And she knew he was evil. She could feel that in her bones.

◦

"You think he's blowing you off?" Stella kicked off her knee-high leather boots and rested her heels on my coffee table. "Why would he do that? I mean, look at you. You're a freaking goddess."

I shrugged. Mr. Charming stood on his perch near the TV and picked at his leg feathers while Cooper sprawled out on the couch next to Stella. He'd just finished dinner and was headed straight for a tuna coma. Pure bliss for him. Stella ran her fingers across his soft fur absentmindedly. "I heard he's hiring a new deputy chief. Maybe he had to interview someone?"

Cooper snuggled closer to his new favorite human. He'd grown more attached to her recently because she brought him cans of Chicken of the Sea every time she visited. I called her a suck-up but she didn't care.

The way to a cat familiar's heart was definitely tuna.

Her relationship with Mr. Charming was another story. She'd tried to get him to bond with her, but he wasn't having any of it, at least not to the degree she wanted. I told her parrots are different; they only bond with one or two humans. Mr. Charming was my mom's parrot, and since her passing, his relationships with Bessie and me had grown, but that was about all the little green god could handle in the emotional department. None of that stopped Stella from trying, though. Since Mr. Charming loved berries, she was constantly stuffing his bowl with raspberries and blackberries, even going as far as to pick them herself during the season. Her efforts were appreciated, but they didn't bring him any closer to a true committed bird and woman relationship.

She eyed him on his perch. "He hates me."

"He doesn't hate you. He's playing hard to get." I sank into the couch on the other side of Cooper. "Maybe that's what Gabe's doing?"

"Maybe he's in love with the new deputy chief he's hiring?" She smirked.

"Funny."

"Can't rule it out."

"Is it a girl?"

She shrugged. "I feel so bad for Doc. He said he lost everything today."

"At least he finally went digital."

"True, but all those supplies." She twisted a loose strand of her long hair around her finger. "I hope this doesn't shut him down."

"It won't. The people in town won't let that happen."

Magicals needed doctors too, especially magical doctors. We got sick just like humans. In fact, I had a serious bout of the stomach flu a few months ago, and if not for Doc, I probably would have been locked in the bathroom for months.

Praise the man for his commitment to modern medicine.

"Anyway, about this new deputy chief."

"You know more about it than I do," I said.

"I know. I've met the guy."

That piqued my interest, almost getting me to sit up straighter. "Do tell."

"I ran into him and Gabe at Eddie's today."

"Gabe went to Eddie's with him?" That was where we were supposed to go. Why did I feel cheated? It was business, and I shouldn't let that bother me. Even though it kind of did anyway.

Stella saw my pouty lips and laughed. "You really like this guy, don't you?"

I twisted a strand of my hair into a braid and let it hang down next to my ear. It slowly loosened and unraveled on its own. "I can't decide."

"Right. That's why you're whining and look like someone just stole your box of Thin Mints." She laughed.

"I love my Thin Mints."

"You're jealous because your sort-of boyfriend is spending time with someone that isn't you!" She waved her hand above her head. "Girl, you've got to get that under control."

Don't I know it. "Anyway," I said, doing my best to change the subject. "I'm stuck in my manuscript. Think you can give me some editorial advice?"

She shifted her body toward me. "Whoa." She pressed her hand to my forehead. "Are you ill?"

I batted her hand away. "I'm serious."

"Fine. Get her, and tell me what's up."

I opened my laptop and showed her my synopsis. "I feel like it's dragging here."

She read through the entire twenty-page document in three minutes flat. Stella was a speed reader, a skill she'd acquired in college. "Okay, I see your point. You need to bring the warlock in sooner. Go back here and have him stop by the coffee shop, maybe? And make him flirt with her. If he acts interested, she can deny the danger he gives off, or maybe confuse it with excitement? What do you think?"

"I like it. So, you think she needs to be interested in him so she can't see he's dangerous? A love-is-blind kind of thing?"

Stella nodded. "One hundred percent. I mean, witches in love should be blind like us humans, right?"

CHAPTER 2

I stayed up late rewriting sections of the book. The good thing about writing is that you can go back and add or delete things to improve your story. The bad thing about writing is you can go back and add or delete things to improve your story. Sometimes, a writer does that so much the story never gets finished. I'm working on a thriller now—shh, it's a secret—and I'm forty thousand words in, but the darn main character hasn't even gotten to the good stuff because I keep adding and deleting scenes. I've been feeling the urge to write under my own name and it's a little more intense than a simple cozy. Not that I'll ever publish it, but maybe.

The man wasn't your average, run-of-the-mill guy. Younger than she'd expected, and Esmerelda was surprised to see the small gray sprigs dotting his hairline. She found it sexy, and loved how it highlighted his ocean-blue eyes. Dark-haired, blue-eyed men practically bled sex appeal, and no human or witch could resist that.

When he walked into the small café, heads turned. Priscilla Ottle-meyer, a witch with a thing for attractive men, sashayed over to the stranger and leaned her hip against the counter beside him. "You new in town?"

Esmerelda wanted to barf. Didn't the witch have a better line than that? The man turned his tall, muscular body toward Priscilla and smiled. Esmerelda nearly melted like the wicked witch in The Wizard of Oz.

I felt like I was writing a romance instead of a cozy, but the setup was important for the inevitable fallout.

"Yes, ma'am. I'm working on a special assignment." He smiled. "Top secret."

Esmerelda winced. Even though the man was attractive, something in his tone sent her intuition into overdrive. Everything about him said stay away, yet something deep within her knew that wasn't possible.

Blah, I thought. Too much wannabe sexual tension. Cozy readers would hit the author hard in the review department about that, but it was necessary for Esmerelda to be fooled. Hopefully when the climax came, they'd realize that.

I checked my phone exactly fifteen times for messages from Gabe, but he hadn't sent a text or even accidentally butt-dialed me.

Cooper eyed me from across my small family room. "Maybe he's not the one."

I kept my eyes glued to my phone. "I never said he was."

"I'm just saying, looks like the dude ain't all that into you."

"You need to stop binge-watching Netflix. Your vocabulary is horrible."

"If you had more excitement in your life, maybe I could."

Ouch.

"Listen, cats know things, you know? And I know when a guy isn't interested. Cats are the kings of uninterested."

"I'm not discussing my romantic life with you."

"Why not? We're intimately connected, and like I said, I know things, especially about you."

I cringed. Adjusting to my cat speaking English was challenging, but I'd done pretty well. Diving into psychobabble about my love life, though, felt intrusive and icky. "You need boundaries."

"Maybe, but our apartment is small, so that's not easy."

I went back to my fictional world and ignored my talking cat.

Before going to bed, I reread the changes I'd made to Esmerelda's story, and though parts of it bordered on clean romance, I was satisfied with what I'd written.

~

I walked through the back door of The Enchanted and smelled snickerdoodles. When I peeked into the small oven, I saw a dozen of them fluffing into warm, chewy goodness. I checked the timer. Five minutes to go. The smell made me want to eat them right away, so I left the kitchen as fast as I could. I only had so much willpower.

Bessie was busy redesigning the display window with a scene from my latest book. Everyone in Holiday Hills knew I was a writer, but they didn't know what I wrote, or that the fake author's books that always reached number one on the *USA Today* best-seller list were mine. She got all the credit, but I got a big portion of the royalties, so I couldn't complain. I poured myself a cup of coffee from the pot behind the counter. I knew from the smell it wasn't magical. Sometimes Bessie liked to add a potion to the pot, but not today.

Bessie's magical thing was helping others help themselves, so I figured no one really needed the extra boost, or I'd be sipping something she'd concocted to bring out their motivations.

I glanced at the empty chairs by the window display, now representing so much tragedy and loss. It was awful not seeing Merlock and Peter anymore, but things happened for a reason, and we'd all done our best to move on. Even Mr. Charming refused to perch his green bundle of love on their backs. Bessie left them there, hoping time would lessen the pain.

The door opened and a tall, muscular man walked in. He wore a black business suit with a deep burgundy tie. His black wingtip shoes were perfectly polished and matched his dark hair. He glanced in my direction, and my breath caught in my throat. If I stood, he'd still tower over me.

His presence, and his confidence, commanded attention. He kept his shoulders back and his head up, and his eyes touched every other set in the room. He exuded power and authority, and he knew it.

A second later the door opened again, and Gabe walked in. He smiled at me, then approached the well-dressed man. A pat on the back and a laugh between the two told me they shared a level of comfort.

Who was the guy? The new deputy chief? If that was the case, he'd sure overdressed for the part. Bessie rushed to the counter and gave them coffees on the house. She caught me gaping at the two and winked.

Gabe walked over, the man following. "Abby, this is Austin Reynolds, Holiday Hills's new deputy chief of police." He turned toward the man. "This is Abby Odell."

I noticed wisps of gray hair intermixed in the dark. They didn't make him look older; instead, they seemed premature. And sexy.

Cooper rubbed his head against my calf. Mr. Charming flew over and landed on my shoulder. I jerked when he dug his nails into my skin.

Austin eyed the bird before smiling at me. "Nice to meet you, Miss Odell."

"It's Abby, please. Nice to meet you too. Welcome to Holiday Hills. If you're a coffee drinker, you're in the right place. Bessie makes the best stuff in town."

"Good to know," he said. "If you'll excuse me, I'm an avid reader, and I'd like to check out the shelves."

I nodded.

Gabe and I shared another awkward moment.

Stella charged in, breaking the silence. "I love it!" She stopped dead in her tracks when she saw Austin Reynolds. "Oh my lawd."

Gabe's eyes shifted to my best friend and then to his new deputy chief before he smiled. "She loves what, exactly?"

"I emailed some changes I made to the novel last night. Changes she recommended."

Stella gawked at Austin, then turned all kinds of red, rushed over, and slunk down in the chair to hide herself behind her laptop.

I laughed.

When the men left—without so much as an "I'll call you later" from Gabe—I refilled my coffee and got her one, too.

"Thought you saw him at Eddie's yesterday?"

"Uh, no."

"But he's the new deputy chief."

"Abs, trust me, if I saw him, I'd definitely remember."

I furrowed my brow. "Maybe he chose someone else."

"Yeah, a former runway model. Did you see the pecs on that man?"

Sometimes Stella was a teeny bit overdramatic.

"He's nice-looking, I'll give him that."

She pursed her lips. "Nice-looking? That's it? The man oozes sex appeal." She flipped open her laptop and pounded on the keys. "I have some thoughts on your WIP."

WIP was writer speak for work in progress, or manuscript. Stella had the literary world jargon down.

Mr. Charming greeted her with a peck at her skull. "Hello there, Mr. Charming. Hello there."

"He's trying to eat my hair."

"He's showing you affection. Isn't that what you've wanted?"

She leaned her head away from him as he rested on her shoulder. "He smells."

"He's a bird."

"A smelly one."

I shook my head. "I give up. What're your thoughts?"

She continued tapping on the keyboard. "I just sent you the file."

I checked my email and opened the document. After reading through her notes, I said, "This is great. Thank you so much."

She eyed her screen. "Weird, though, isn't it?"

"What?"

"The mystery man you described looks just like that new guy." She practically swooned. "Maybe you're psychic?"

Bessie glanced at me, her eyebrow raised ever so slightly.

"Nah, I'm just your average witch." My eyes popped. "I mean, Esmerelda's just your average witch."

Stella laughed. "I'm not saying they're real or not, but if they are, you're definitely not one." She crossed her legs. "You're way too wishy-washy."

Bessie chuckled.

"I'm not wishy-washy."

"I like Gabe. I don't like Gabe. I'm writing under my name. I'm not writing under my name. I'm buying a new car. I'm not buying a new car." She grinned. "See? Wishy-washy."

"Big decisions take time."

"Exactly how much time do you need?"

I smiled. "I need time to figure that out too."

"You're hopeless," Stella continued. "There's a weird déjà vu thing going on with your character and the new hottie in town."

I crossed and uncrossed my ankles. She was right, and I'd learned enough about witchcraft and the universe to know nothing was coincidental. A shared look, a stranger's smile, a windy cold day during the summer—it all led to something. We may not understand or even know the reasons, but they were there, and they had purpose. An uneasy feeling came over me, filling me with angst, but I brushed it aside. "It's my amazing writing skills. I can make stuff happen just by writing it down."

She shrugged. "You've always been a little weird."

That was truer than she knew. My cell phone dinged with a text. I pulled it from my bag and clicked on the messages icon, and my heartbeat kicked into the anaerobic zone when I saw it was from Gabe.

Sorry about yesterday. I needed to fill the position, and I had a meeting with my top candidate yesterday, but he backed out at the last minute. I just didn't want to discuss that in front of Reynolds. Dinner later tonight?

Stella read my mind. "Gabe, right?"

I nodded. "He wants to go to dinner tonight."

"Well, are you going to respond?"

I tapped on the screen and hit send.

"Can't make it tonight. Deadline looming," I told her.

Her eyes widened. "Look at you playing all hard to get!"

"Not really. I do have a deadline, and I need to get moving."

I spent the rest of the day and evening working on Esmerelda's adventure, and when Bessie finally kicked me out as she headed to lock the door, I decided to take a walk down the street and pick up a slice of pizza for dinner. I was too mentally exhausted to cook, and pizza hit all four food groups, so it was basically healthy.

I took the long route to the pizza place. I loved walking in town. The cool night air was good for me mentally and physically, and I liked the view. Several stores had prepared for the season with pumpkins and corn stalks and all things fall. Agatha Messer changed up the little bundles of hay outside her store, Agatha's Antiques, daily. Tonight's display featured two antique dolls wearing off-white dresses and admiring themselves in an old-fashioned mirror. As I walked by, I thought one of them winked at me, so I kicked up my speed and darted across the street.

Frieda and Starling Starlight owned Starlight Gifts, a charming women's fashion boutique across from the antique store. A few weeks ago I bought a muted green and cream knit scarf there, and I couldn't wait to wear it. I slowed as I walked past their display, practically drooling at the mannequin's beige leather boots and cream sweater. I'd be making another trip inside soon for sure.

Cooper sauntered behind me, complaining about his lack of treats throughout the day and requesting a new cloth mouse filled with kitty pot. His word choice, not mine. "It makes me chill, and living with you, I need to be chill."

"Catnip does not make you chill. It makes you crazy hyper and then crash and snore."

"I have a small nose. It gets stuffed easily."

"If you'd like, I can stick a Q-tip in it and clean it out."

He flinched, then raced ahead of me, meowing what I suspected were kitty curse words along the way. The cat has issues.

When I caught up to him, he was standing at the entrance to the alley near the pizza shop at the far end of downtown Holiday Hills. He hissed, and I stared into the alley, seeing Austin Reynolds walking out of the pizza place's side door. I ducked around the corner and peeped toward him, hoping he couldn't feel the power of my stare burning into his well-dressed back.

He stopped with his back facing me for a second and then slowly turned around, smiling.

Busted.

As he walked toward me, my heart raced.

"I don't like this dude," Cooper said.

I shushed him. Thankfully, Bessie brought Mr. Charming home or Goddess only knew what he'd do. Mr. Charming wasn't very subtle when he didn't like someone. Cooper wasn't all that subtle either, but he held it together for the time being.

"Ms. Odell, yes?"

"Uh, I...yes, sir. Deputy Chief, I mean."

He laughed. "You can call me Austin."

I shifted my weight from one foot to the other. "Oh, then please, call me Abby."

"Abby it is." He stared at Cooper, who'd settled prominently in front of me. "And your cat?"

I glanced down and picked him up. "Isn't very social," I said as Cooper hissed. "But his name's Cooper."

He eyed my familiar, and the hair down Cooper's spine stood at attention. "Interesting breed."

"He's a Burmese." I hoisted him up so his head rested on my shoulder. "They're called silky bricks because their hair is soft and they're so dense."

Cooper turned his head and stared at me. "Hey now, who you calling dense?"

My eyes widened, and I glanced over at Austin. "I was just…I, uh…I was just getting a slice of pizza." Yes, that's me, Abby Odell, conversationalist extraordinaire. The wordsmith. Not at all awkward.

"I could use another. How about I buy? You can fill me in on the inner workings of Holiday Hills from a citizen's point of view."

Wasn't he just leaving? "Uh, sure. I can do that."

We sat at one of the small wood tables. He drank a beer, and I had a Diet Coke. I tapped my toes on the painted cement table, wondering if my nerves were because of his attractiveness or the uneasy air about him. As we waited for our pizza slices—which took an unusually long time—he quizzed me on Holiday Hills. "Where do you spend most of your time?"

"What do you mean?"

"Places in town. Where do you like to go?"

"You met me at my favorite spot this morning."

He nodded. "The Enchanted, yes. Strange name for a bookstore, don't you think?"

I raised a brow. "Books transport people to other places and times. I'd say that's enchanting."

"That could be true. That fire at the doctor's office. Were you one of his patients?"

I nodded as I sipped my Diet Coke.

"You'll have to find another?"

"Why would I do that? Doc will find another space soon enough, and I just had a physical a few months ago. I'm sure he'll have a place by the time I need another."

"What if something happens and you need a doctor before then?"

"I'm a pretty healthy person. I don't expect to get sick anytime soon."

"That flu going around is pretty brutal."

"Been there, done that."

"What about other places? Is there someplace you like to go to relax or take a breather?"

"Holiday Hills."

He smiled. "Can you be more specific?"

"Why do I feel like I'm being interrogated?"

He relaxed back in his chair. "I'm sorry. Old habits die hard, I guess."

I changed the subject. "What brings you to Holiday Hills?"

"Besides the job?"

I smiled. "Where are you from?"

"Most recently, Chicago."

The cashier brought our two slices of pizza on flimsy paper plates. I cut mine with my plastic knife, almost tearing through the plate. "Chicago, huh? You'll probably be bored here, then."

"I have a feeling I'll be just as busy here."

Sirens blared in the distance. We pivoted toward the front of the restaurant as the cashier rushed out. "Another fire! There's another fire!"

I jumped from my seat. "What? Where?"

"Jeremiah Remmington just texted me," the young woman said. "It's your momma's old house, Abby. It's burning down!"

I rushed toward the door, then zipped back around and grabbed my purse before sprinting outside. Cooper raced behind me. Once around the corner and out of sight, I imagined my mom's old Victorian cottage and pushed my finger into my nose. "Take me there," I whispered, though it felt more like a prayer.

Cooper latched onto my leg just in time, and poof! We were standing outside my mother's home, watching the flames engulf her small front porch and the old rocking chair I'd left for the new owners. I wanted that chair, but their little girl had loved it so much, I didn't have the heart to take it from her.

A fireman shoved me out of his way. "Ma'am, you can't be here." He pointed toward the street. "It's safer over there."

I stepped back, and he took off, hose in hand, rushing closer to my mother's ruined home.

All the memories. All the secrets. All the life lived in that old home. Gone.

Everything burned until the place was a scattering of charred furniture, burned walls, and an almost-collapsed roof. I leaned against the mailbox and sobbed. In less than a year I'd lost so much.

A gentle hand massaged my shoulder. It was warm and comforting, and it seemed natural to lean toward the person attached to it. When the voice whispered in my ear, telling me things would be okay, I stiffened.

It wasn't Gabe. It was Austin.

I stared at what was left of my mom's old home, watched the firemen aim their hoses at the smoldering ash, spraying away the foundation of my life. Gabe stood near the burned mess, his eyes locked on me. I wiped mine and rubbed my nose, and a frog appeared at my feet. "Not now," I told the frog. I rubbed under my nose, and he disappeared.

Funny how the things in my subconscious sneak in real time. I'd spent one summer fascinated by frogs. At night, my mother and I would sit on the front porch listening to them in the trees, and every once in a while, one would pop onto the porch and smile at us. So many memories being washed away by the firemen.

Gabe walked over, and I rushed into his welcoming arms, sobbing about all the things I'd lost. I felt secure and safe with his arms around me. Why, then, did a foreboding feeling wash over me?

An hour later I sat on my couch, stunned, confused, and scared. "Something's happening. I can feel it."

Cooper propped himself up beside me. "I'm with you on that."

I looked down at him. "It's not good."

"I'm with you on that too."

~

Bessie's eyes were swollen and blood-red. "Oh honey," she said when I walked in. She pulled me to her. "I can't imagine how you're feeling." She let go after almost crushing my ribs.

Mr. Charming flew over and perched on my left shoulder. "I love you, Mr. Charming. I love you."

I smiled at his way of expressing love. "I love you too, Mr. Charming."

He nibbled on my hair.

Cooper sat on the counter next to the register, eyeing Bessie as if he hadn't eaten in days and she was his next meal. She noticed and rushed behind the counter for a bag of tuna. She kept a stash there for these kinds of emergencies. One rip of the top later and cranky Coop had his late gourmet breakfast in his little glass bowl.

I'd stopped feeding him on the mornings I went to The Enchanted. He'd gained three pounds, and for a cat who shouldn't weigh more than nine, those extra three pounds weighed him down. Literally. He made num-num sounds while he scarfed down his breakfast.

"How're you holding up?" she asked.

I shrugged. "I've been better."

"And worse, that we know."

I was all for looking on the positive side of things, but I needed some time to think, to get my head straight before walking around saying things like, *it was just a house.* I set my bag on the table while she poured me a cup of coffee. A heavy sigh escaped my lips.

"Here, it's got a dollop of happiness in it just for you."

"Can you make it two dollops? I feel like I need the extra."

She smiled, then waved her hand over the cup. "Done."

Normally I'd sit and chat, but I wasn't feeling it. Besides, I was behind on my deadline, so writing took priority over feeling sorry for myself.

I opened the file for my work in progress. I'd stopped at a pivotal point where Esmerelda cast a spell on the arsonist, hoping it would stop him from setting any more fires. I scrolled down to the end of the file, and then back up two pages. I always read the last few pages before starting again. Even though I had a synopsis, I needed the refresher to get my creative muse going.

I stared at the words on the screen and blinked. Then I blinked again.

The fire engulfed the small house, sending sparks of yellow and red flames into the night sky and lighting it up like the Fourth of July fireworks finale. The roof caved, crashing down with a loud boom and sending a wave of heat so strong toward Esmerelda that she ducked her head into her arm.

"No," she screamed. "No!"

A soft hand pressed her shoulder, then gripped tightly and pulled her close to a warm yet comforting body. She cried into a soft cotton shirt, desperately trying to cast away the flames.

"It'll be okay," the familiar voice whispered.

I couldn't stop reading the words on the screen. How had this happened? I didn't write that, and it was almost exactly what happened to me. "No. No. No. No."

Bessie rushed from behind the counter, and Cooper jumped onto the table, sticking his face around the side of the screen.

"What's wrong?"

"That's not good," Cooper said.

My eyes widened. "You can read that?"

"Been practicing."

I angled my laptop toward Bessie. "This."

She read the screen, and her eyes bulged. "Why are you writing about the fire?"

"I'm not. I...I didn't."

She pulled out the chair next to me and stared at me. "Then how? Oh, dear."

"What? Why oh dear?"

Stella walked in, darted toward me, and wrapped her arms around my shoulders, jerking my head toward her flat stomach. I couldn't breathe. "Oh sweetie, I'm so sorry."

Bessie caught my eye and closed my laptop as Stella released me from her death grip. I rubbed my neck. She had some seriously strong forearms.

"I heard the news this morning. I couldn't believe it. They think it's arson. Two fires now. What's going on?"

That was my question too, on so many levels. First the similarities between seeing the man in the alley—or, in my case, seeing Austin Reynolds in the alley—and now the fire? Something, or someone, was sending me a message. But what? And why?

CHAPTER 3

*B*essie offered Stella a cup of coffee, but I gave her mine.

She tilted her head. "I thought you wanted that?"

"May I have a tea instead? Just regular old tea, nothing special." I hoped she got the hint. I needed perspective, a clear state of mind instead of a happy fog, and the double dollop of magic sent me toward the latter. I should have known that would happen.

Stella, on the other hand, high-strung as she could be, deserved a little happy.

"Oh, I'll take a tea too. It feels like that kind of day." She continued to babble about the fire, and I did my best to pretend I was okay. Only, I wasn't. I was a hot mess.

"Earth to Abby."

I blinked.

Stella leaned closer. "You there?"

Cooper rubbed his head against my calf.

"I'm here. Sorry."

She reached across the table and squeezed my hand. "You have nothing to be sorry about. "It's been a tough year for you, and now this? You need a vacation."

What I needed was to figure out what the heck was going on.

"How's the writing going? Are you able to concentrate?"

"I have to. Deadlines don't just disappear."

She smiled. "Then I'll let you get to it." She dunked her tea bag in and out of her cup. "I've got a meeting in Atlanta, but if you need me, I can stick around."

"I appreciate that, but it's okay. I'm a big girl."

"I know, but I'm your best friend. I feel like I should be here for you."

"You are, and I appreciate it, but I'm fine. I promise."

She angled her head and examined me carefully. "Okay, then I guess I'm out of here." She stood and squeezed me into a tight hug, nearly choking me again. "If you need me, you know how to reach me."

"You're not going away forever."

"You never know. I might meet the man of my dreams and not come back."

A bolt of internal electricity zipped down my spine. "Don't say that," I blurted out.

She laughed. "As if I'd ever leave you!"

Bessie shot me a look, and I glanced down so my expression wouldn't give me away. Stella said goodbye, and as she walked out, Gabe walked in. My body temperature rose.

He offered me a sad smile. "How you holding up?"

"I'm fine," I lied.

"Hey there, Chief. You want your usual?" Bessie asked.

"That would be great, Bess. Thanks."

He eyed my closed laptop. "Writer's block?"

"I think I need to go for a walk. My creative muse needs some fresh air."

He raised an eyebrow.

"It's a writer thing. Not a split personality." Why did he

always make me so nervous? "So," I said, changing the subject, "Stella said the fire department thinks the fire was arson?"

He nodded. "Fire chief and I are meeting in an hour to discuss. We think one person is responsible for the fire at Doc's and your mother's old house."

"Is there a way to tell?"

"There is, and I'll let you know what we find out."

"I'd appreciate it."

He stared at me so hard I squirmed in my seat. "I'd still like to spend some time with you. Dinner tonight? I can update you on what we find out."

I nodded. "Sure, that would be great."

"It might be late. How about my place, around eight? I'll pick up Italian."

My stomach did a little cha-cha. "Uh, sure. Sounds good."

He smiled and placed his hand on my shoulder. "I'm really sorry about your mom's place, Ab."

A clap of thunder and a bolt of lightning sent me inches off my seat. "That was loud."

Gabe stared out the picture window. My eyes followed. I watched as Ryland Augustus stared into the bookstore, then slowly turned and walked away.

～

The man whispered in Esmerelda's ear, "He can't keep you safe. I'll get what I've come for."

She pushed him away, the scent of his woody cologne lingering against her skin. "You won't win," she said, then stood and walked toward the door. "I won't let you." Her legs shook as she walked, but Esmerelda wouldn't let him win. She couldn't. The fires. She would stop him. She had to, because if she lost, no one she loved would be safe. She would not let him win.

"You think you can beat me." He laughed. "You're a fool. I didn't *come this far, sacrifice this much, to lose. I'll do what it takes to get what I came for, Abby."*

The words typed themselves. I stared at the screen as my fingers hit letters that didn't match the words on my screen.

I froze as the sentence typed itself over and over on the page.

I'll do what it takes to get what I came for, Abby.

I pounded my finger on the delete key, but just as soon as I erased a line, it reappeared. I beat the key so hard it jarred loose and I had to reset it. I slammed my laptop shut, tossed it into my bag, and asked Bessie to watch Mr. Charming.

"Of course, honey. He's my big sweetie."

"Big sweetie. Big sweetie," the parrot repeated.

I felt awful. I knew my mother would be fine with her parrot spending so much time with her best friend, but he was my responsibility. I just hoped all the back and forth didn't confuse him.

Cooper propped up on his bum and said, "I'm coming."

I was halfway to the door before he finished stretching.

He was breathing heavily when he caught up. "Geez, what's the rush?"

"I'm being threatened in my story."

"Wait—what?"

I let the door slam without so much as a goodbye and headed to Mystie's Magical Haven, the local potion store. Mystie was a witch with a dash of psychic power. She read cards and auras and let crystals guide her. I had a crystal, but I'd only used it as a pendulum to locate missing things and people.

"Well, hey there, Ab." Mystie smiled and pulled me into a hug. "Goodness, your aura is dark. It's the fire, isn't it?"

I sighed. "That's just part of it."

She nodded. "I'm sorry. I know you loved that house."

"I need help. I think something's going on, and I'm not sure what to do."

She examined me carefully. "Of course, sweetie. Come." She

hooked her finger, and I followed her behind the hanging beads. "Sit."

When Mystie focused, she kept her mind centered and her words few. She held a crystal hanging from a chain over a deck of tarot cards. After a few seconds, she removed the bottom and top cards and set them face down on the table. "Flip them." She paused. "Wait." The crystal pendulum swung over one of the cards. "This one. Turn it over first."

I slowly turned the card over and gasped. "That's the death card!"

She nodded. "Yes, sweetie, but it doesn't mean what you think. Turn over the other card now, please."

I hesitated, but did as she said. "The fool?" I really needed to study these things.

"Again, it's not what you think. Usually the fool means wisdom and strength coupled with new beginnings, but in its reverse position, like yours, it shows a resistance from you." She studied me carefully.

My eyes widened. "Is this about the fires? What would I be resisting? That doesn't make sense."

"Yes, it's about the fires, but I'm feeling more than that. It's you, your energy and actions. You're going to be pushing back harder than you should. You need to understand this is bigger than just you, and you can't do this alone."

"I don't understand."

"Something big is happening. I don't know what, but I know it's about you." She held the crystal over the cards again. "I see a necklace. It holds great magic."

"A magic necklace? Where is it?"

"No, it's not magic." The crystal swung toward the fool card. "It's like a key. You must find that necklace, Abby. It belongs to you." The crystal swung again. "There's more. Something smaller." She closed her eyes and leaned back against her chair. "I can't quite see it, but there's something else you need. You'll find it soon. Keep it safe. Don't let him get it."

"Who? Who's trying to get it?"

"A very angry, selfish being."

"Does he have a name?"

"I…I…" She shook her head. Worry overwhelmed her face, and from the deep furrow of her brow, I knew she was truly afraid for me.

"Do you know who's doing this?"

"Someone you'd least expect. Don't trust anyone, Abby. Especially men."

As if I'd done that in a long time.

Cooper sat next to me on top of the table. His eyes caught mine, and he looked just as worried as me.

～

Cooper and I sat on my couch staring at the book. I'd asked it to help, but it stayed closed. When I tried to physically open it with my hand, it wouldn't budge.

He moved closer to it, tilting his head and examining it more closely. "I got nothin'. It's like you're locked out or something."

"This isn't good, Coop. You heard what Mystie said: something bad's going to happen."

"She didn't say that, Ab. She said you need to get the necklace."

"And something else."

"She didn't say outright something bad would happen."

"No, but she implied it. What if I can't stop it."

He sat next to me on the couch. "You can. We can, and we will." He rubbed his head against my arm. "You're powerful, and I'm, you know, me. We'll figure this out and kick some serious booty."

The side of my mouth twitched. "I appreciate you."

He licked his paw. "As you should." He climbed on top of my lap. "I got your back, Ab. That's my job."

"I know."

My cell phone dinged. I unlocked it and read a text from Gabe. *Seven-thirty okay? I'll grab the food.*

I replied, *Sounds good. I'll bring dessert.*

"I don't know about this," Cooper said.

"What?"

"You heard what Mystie said."

"She wasn't talking about Gabe." Even though I said the words, I wasn't sure I believed them.

"You don't know that for sure."

"Then there's only one way to find out, isn't there?"

He shook his head. "Bringing your cat to a dinner date isn't cool, Abs."

"I wasn't planning on bringing you."

"Plans change."

"Fine, but you're going to have to hang out outside. I don't want him thinking I'm some crazy cat lady who can't go anywhere without you."

"Dude, he's seen you at The Enchanted. With me, and the bird. Duh."

I narrowed my eyes at my familiar. "Just stay outdoors, okay? If I need you, I'll…" I tapped my finger to my chin. "I'll wave my hand in the air. Then you'll know to come in."

"If he's on top of you, you won't be able to wave your hand."

"Coop! I'm not that kind of woman!"

My cat shook his head. "I don't mean it that way. Geez, what are you, a twelve-year-old boy?"

"That's kind of what I think about you." I couldn't help but smile. "Besides, I highly doubt Gabe is involved." Although I wasn't sure I actually believed it.

"Better safe than sorry."

CHAPTER 4

My apartment sat above The Enchanted. It was small, less than eight hundred square feet, but I didn't need more than that. Besides, I loved how cozy it felt. I loved the pale yellow walls, the old built-in bookcases, the creaky wood floors, and even the popcorn ceiling.

Bessie owned the entire building, and the rent was super cheap, which was a plus. I could afford more, but she wouldn't take more from me. I'd put my ex-husband through grad school. While he studied and went to class, I worked my behind off writing articles for various magazines and ghost wrote several business books and autobiographies for businessmen. The work was intense and time-consuming, but my ex was always studying at the school library. Or so I thought. When he graduated and chose to leave me for another woman, a female judge and an excellent attorney decided his fancy job at the CDC was partly because of my efforts. I'd received a lump sum in our divorce. My mother also left me money I hadn't expected, my agent had recently negotiated a high-paying ghostwriting contract for me, and my compensation doubled for each Esmerelda book.

I wasn't suffering financially at all, but I didn't see the need to spend the money on another place when I was happy where I was.

What I did spend the money on was good food, especially dessert. After showering and putting on a cute pair of Silver Jeans, a white cable knit sweater with a black camisole underneath, and a pair of black leather boots, I was good to go…to the grocery store for brownies.

I'd make my own, but I liked Gabe a lot and didn't want to unintentionally poison him. Cooking wasn't my thing.

When we arrived at Gabe's house, Cooper scurried off to the corner of the front porch and nestled comfortably in one of two rocking chairs. "Wave your hand or scream if you need me."

"Yeah, because you won't be snoring in a minute."

Gabe opened the front door just then. "I'm sorry, I didn't hear you."

I blushed. "No worries, I was talking to myself."

He smiled and moved to the side. "Come on in."

Every time I went to his place, my heart raced and my palms sweated. I was still nervous around him, and even more so when outside my normal environments. My ex damaged my trust in men, and as kind and honest as Gabe seemed, I didn't trust him completely. It wasn't his fault, but at some point, I'd either have to take a leap of faith or walk away. His issues weren't the only reason our relationship wasn't moving forward.

I had to push all that aside for the time being and focus on the fires. Mystie told me to watch myself, to not trust men. She didn't say which men specifically, and I needed to figure out if she meant Gabe. Could he be involved? He was human, not magical. But then again, Mystie didn't say the person responsible for the fires was a magical. Could this necklace hold power, and if so, did a human know about it?

Some humans believed in magic, and it was possible for them to discover our secret. No system was perfect, right? The only thing I could do was spend time with Gabe and see what I discovered. He never gave any signs of being magical, and if he knew that I was a witch, he hadn't let on. So if he was magical, why wouldn't others know? What possible reason would he have for hiding that?

Because he wanted to fool me. That's why.

On the outside, Gabe's house was a traditional post-Civil War-era replica. It was adorable, with white painted bricks, large columns, and a matching white cement front porch. The black shutters accentuated the large windows, and the red door was my favorite part. The inside, though, was somewhat of a surprise. He'd gutted the entire place and modernized it to one of those straight-line designs. Deceptively traditional on the outside, but something completely different on the inside.

He poured me a glass of white wine. Since discovering my witchy self, I'd pretty much given up wine or any kind of alcohol. A lot of nose scratching happened when I was tipsy, and one time, while hanging out with Stella, I'd sent her goldfish soaring across her family room and straight into her fireplace. Thank goodness she hadn't seen it happen, but let me tell you, it freaked me out.

That fish hadn't looked at me since, either. Animals could see the magic in the world, and he hated me now.

I sipped the white wine as he finished preparing the pasta. "Wait. I thought you were picking up dinner?"

"I was going to, but I decided to make it myself. I haven't done it in a while, and I was in the mood."

"A man who cooks. I could get used to that."

He smiled. "I'm hoping you will."

My heart raced.

He drained the pasta and poured it into a bowl, then placed it on the table next to the sauce, garlic bread, and salad. "It's not chef inspired, but I make a good sauce."

I smiled and sat across from him. Soft music played in the background, and we chatted while we ate. He kept his eyes focused intently on me, and part of me wanted to sink in my chair and hide under the table.

"I really like what you've done in here," I said.

"You mean the décor?"

"Everything. These homes are so boxy, but you've opened it up nicely. It feels so big."

"Thanks. I've always wanted to redo a place, but I've never had the time."

"So, you didn't do this yourself?"

"I designed it, but no. I had a company do the actual work."

Gabe had lost his wife prior to moving to Holiday Hills, and though we never talked about it, I suspected he'd received money from a life insurance policy. Police chiefs in small towns didn't earn the big bucks, and considering how the house looked, it couldn't have been cheap. Though he could be a saver.

Or a warlock.

I glanced at the front window and saw my cat standing on his hind legs, stalking us.

Gabe caught me staring and flipped around. "Is that your cat?"

I blushed. "He's a little attached."

He laughed, then walked over to the door and opened it. "Come on in, boy."

Cooper sauntered over, gave Gabe a stern examination, then promptly stood at my side.

"He really does seem to watch over you."

I smiled. "My little bodyguard, I guess."

"I don't want to spoil a nice night, but I have some news about the fires."

I set down my fork.

"Austin has some experience with arson, and based on our conversation with the fire chief, it looks like both fires were started with gas cloths."

"Gas cloths?"

He nodded. "Fire department found remnants at both your mom's old house and Doc's place."

"But how could they know? Wouldn't they have burned?"

"We got lucky. There were scraps of them under bricks, so they were saved."

"I don't understand why someone would burn down those two places."

"I was hoping you might have an idea."

I pointed to myself. "Me? What makes you think that?"

He stood and walked over to the kitchen counter, then returned with a large beige envelope. He opened it and removed two photos, one of me at each location. I stared at them, my mouth gaping. Someone had used a zoom lens to take the photos, which meant they'd been watching for me. Or watching me.

"Do you know when these might have been taken?"

I examined the one of me stepping out of Doc's office building. I had on my pink sweatshirt and a pair of black yoga pants. The other was outside my mom's place, while I was chatting with the new owners. I'd gone for a walk and wandered by the house without intending to. I wore the same pink sweatshirt and black yoga pants.

He set the photos on the table. "Whatever you might remember could be important, Abby."

"These were taken last Friday. I had a follow-up appointment at Doc's, and then I…I was struggling with my WIP and I…"

"Your WIP?"

"My manuscript. Work in progress."

He nodded. "Go on."

"I left Doc's office and went for a walk. I wanted to clear my mind, you know, see if I could find some inspiration."

He didn't speak right away, and I felt incredibly uncomfortable. Cooper nuzzled into my lap and closed his eyes. Some help he was.

"I...I don't understand," I said. "How did the photos get there? Wouldn't they have been destroyed in the fires?"

"Not if they were left after the fact. The heat from the charred remains could have ignited the photos. But Abby, that's not the only thing." He removed two partially burned papers from the envelope. "Read these."

Cooper propped up on my lap and read them with me. I knew he could read, but I hoped Gabe wouldn't notice and question it.

I read the first one. *I'm coming for her.* The second one said the same thing, only with an added, *I will get what I desire.*

Cooper said, "Crap."

I dropped the papers on the table and sighed.

Gabe stood and rounded the table, then picked up the photos and letters and stuffed them back into the envelope. "Do you have any idea why someone would write this? What did they mean by getting what they desire?"

Should I tell him what Mystie said? Would he consider it the ramblings of what he thought was a fake psychic? I decided not to. I didn't know if I should trust him. "I don't have a clue." I twisted a chunk of hair around my finger. "I can't think of anyone I've had any issues with lately either."

"That was my next question. What about the book you're writing? Would the publisher or the author have an issue with it?"

My book? Why would he bring that up? Did he know it was writing itself? Was he a magical? Mystie's words echoed in my mind. *Don't trust anyone, Abby. Especially men.* It was possible Gabe was hiding his magical self from me. Being a witch doesn't make me all-knowing.

I still had so much to learn about the magical world. Bessie did her best to teach me, but witchcraft was centuries old, and we'd barely touched the surface. Gabe, Stella, and virtually everyone I knew could be hiding their magic from me and I'd have no way of knowing.

But other than something nefarious like hurting me or trying to take my powers, what reason would they have for hiding from me? It wouldn't be the first time. I've been told I'm a very powerful witch, but sneezing and sending fish flying into the air doesn't make me feel all that powerful. I was magically stronger than before, and it was possible the necklace could heighten my abilities even more so. It was also possible someone else would want the necklace for their own power boost. If that was even possible. But Gabe? Could he be the one doing it?

We spent the rest of the evening discussing how to proceed, and our ideas clashed. I wanted to use magic to figure it out myself, which I didn't tell him, of course. He wanted to go the law enforcement route, but if this was a magical issue, I wasn't sure they could help.

When I stood to leave, Gabe stood too. He held my shoulder. "Austin's got experience in private security. I'd like to have him keep an eye on you."

"Keep an eye on me?"

He nodded. "Listen, one of two things is happening here. Either the person who set the fire left the notes, or the person who left the notes is taking advantage of the fires. I'm leaning toward the first, and with Austin close by, we can find out."

I shook my head. "I don't think I need...I'm not comfortable with that."

"He knows what he's doing." His kind and concerned eyes eased my distrust. "We'll get through this, Abby. I won't let anything happen to you."

CHAPTER 5

It was past midnight, but I wasn't tired. I was tense and anxious, and the last thing I wanted to do was go home and try to sleep. I drove to what was left of my mother's house, lowered the car window, and stared at the blackened debris. Memories flooded my heart, and the tightness in my chest made it feel impossible to breathe. "Oh, Mom. I wish you were here. I need help."

A black car slowed to a stop behind me. I gripped my steering wheel as Cooper hissed. The car lights flashed and then turned off, and the driver's side door opened. I kicked my car into drive and eased my foot off the brake, letting the car roll forward a bit.

"Abby? Is that you?"

I recognized the voice and posture of the shadow walking toward my car. I hit the brake hard and the car jerked to a stop.

Ryland appeared at the window, leaning in toward me. "You okay?"

"I'm, uh, good. What're you doing out so late?" And how did he know my car?

"I could ask you the same thing."

"I'm on my way home from a friend's."

He raised an eyebrow. "Stella?"

I shook my head. "No, someone else."

He smiled. "Is she seeing someone?"

"Stella? Not at the moment, but I'm not sure she's—"

"Great. I was thinking of asking her out. Think I should?"

"I guess. I was just going to say I'm not sure she's interested in dating at the moment. She's pretty busy with work."

"Won't hurt to ask."

"True."

He flicked his head toward the house. "It was your mom's house, right?"

I nodded and stepped out of my car, first giving Cooper a quick, inconspicuous thumbs up. "Yes." I closed the door behind me and leaned against it. "It's strange, you know, seeing it like this."

His eyes softened as he stared at what was left of the home. "I can't even begin to imagine." He leaned next to me. "Anyone say how it happened?"

"Fire."

His eyes shifted my direction, and I could tell he wasn't sure if I was being sarcastic. "I mean, what started the fire?"

I shrugged. "I'm not sure. I sold the house months ago, so if the fire department knows, I don't know if they'll tell me."

"Seems a little coincidental, happening almost right after the fire at the doctor's office. I'd say arson."

He was right. It was a little too coincidental, and most people would think the same, so why was the hair on the back of my neck sticking straight up?

"I've learned anything's possible," I said.

He glued his eyes to the burned remains of my happy memories. "It's late. You want me to follow you home?"

"It's okay. I don't live far."

"You're in the apartment above The Enchanted, right? Really, it's no trouble at all."

For a guy who was pretty new in town, he sure knew a lot. "Thanks, but it's okay."

We said our goodbyes, and Cooper stared at me as I drove the short distance back to our place.

"What?"

"Don't you think that's odd?"

"You mean Ryland showing up like that and offering to drive me home?"

"Yup, that."

"It's also strange that he knows so much about stuff already. Like, how would he know where I live?"

"Google."

I rolled my eyes. "That's my point. Why the interest? And he immediately suggested the fires are arson."

"I'm just a cat, but I think most people would think that after two fires in a short time."

"True, but something doesn't feel right to me." I tapped my fingers on the steering wheel as I turned onto my street. "I don't trust him."

"New guy in town. Shows up out of nowhere. Things burn down. He follows you late at night. Nah, he's good." He stared at me like the Grumpy Cat that used to be all over the internet. "Duh."

"I'm on the same page as you."

"Maybe it's time we do a little internet search of our own, see what we can find out about Mr. Makes Women Swoon."

"I wouldn't go that far."

"Then how about Mr. Makes Stella Swoon?"

I smiled. "Is that jealousy I hear in your tone?"

He shook his head. "She's sort of part of the package, you know? I protect you. She's your best friend. See my point?"

"Em hmm." He was definitely put off by Ryland, and definitely jealous. I stared up at my kitchen window. The overhead light was left on, something I never did. I pointed to it. "Do you see that?"

"Oh, that might be my fault."

"The light switch is four feet from the floor, and *you* left it on?"

He pivoted toward me and then back to the window. "Oh, my bad. Thought you were talking about the ripped screen."

I squinted for a better look. "When did you do that?"

"I'm not really tuned into time like you."

I stared at him.

He propped up on his hind legs and held up his front paws in surrender. "Fine, fine. I smelled those hot tuna things Bessie was making the other morning, and I got hungry. You were being lazy, sleeping in, and you know, a cat's got to do what a cat's got to do."

"Hot tuna things? You mean tuna melts? You ate one of those?"

"Ew, no. Hot tuna is all kinds of wrong. I got me a can of it nice and lukewarm and still soaking in the water. Bessie loves me."

I swallowed hard. Tuna wasn't one of my favorite foods. "I love you too, and I get you the good stuff all the time."

"I wouldn't say all the time."

"Whatever."

We climbed out of the car, completely forgetting about the light in my kitchen.

Cooper flicked his head toward the window. "You really think I could reach the light switch with these stubs?" He kicked out his back leg.

My familiar has short leg syndrome, or SLS for short. His legs, adorable as they are, are shorter than the length of my hands. I feel for the guy. Jumping six inches is a big deal for him, and he was right: there was no way he could have flicked that switch. Which meant someone else did.

Cooper might be small, but he's mighty and muscular, and when his little paws hit the ground, they sound like a bowling ball rolling down an alley. He doesn't know how to be quiet. I, on the other hand, could be, so I swept him up in my arms and tiptoed up the stairs to my apartment.

My door, which I'm positive I closed and locked, was open.

Cooper wiggled out of my grasp and thumped to the ground. "Well, crap."

I flicked the tip of my finger across my nose and the walls to my place disappeared in my mind's eye.

I checked every corner, every closet—I only had two—under the bed, behind the couch, and under the tables. While I saw nothing concerning, Cooper wanted to make sure, and he bolted in, doing his own cursory scatter-through just in case.

"All clear," he hollered from inside.

I set my keys on the table and shuffled to the kitchen to get a bottle of water and turn off the light. "The window's open?"

Cooper sauntered in. "Wha—"

"The window's open! I didn't see that when I checked the apartment." I pulled it closed. "And the screen is gone."

"I'm good but not that good."

I rolled my eyes. "Okay, can we skip with the snark for a moment and get serious?"

"It's how I deal."

We walked to the couch. "The window's not very big. Maybe Stella could fit through it, but anyone bigger would get stuck."

"Your point?"

"I don't think anyone broke in through the window."

"You think it's a diversion?"

"It's the person who took those photos of me, I'm sure of it."

"Which means it's a magical." He pranced toward the book-shelf and eyed the family book. "Or a fairy."

"Fairies are real?"

He laughed. "This is me making a joke. You remember what those are, right?"

"I'm not in a joking mood. If the person doing this is a magical, that means it could be someone posing as a human." I let that thought sink in. "And it could be Gabe."

"It could be anyone. A magical doesn't have to be hiding their supernatural state to be deceptive, Abby. You know that better than anyone."

I couldn't deny that, but I also couldn't shake the feeling that I knew the person, and I possibly knew them well.

The Odell book of magic floated from its spot on the shelf and landed on the coffee table.

Cooper's eyes shot open. "Did you do that?"

I stared at the book as it flipped through pages before finally stopping. "Nope."

He scooted over to the table and stared at the pages. "It never ceases to amaze me how much new stuff shows up in this thing."

I bent close and read the pages carefully. My mouth opened into an O. "This can't be good."

"That's what I'm thinking."

I reread the passage out loud, as if doing that would make it sound less frightening.

"When the fires end, death will happen. What once was strong will be long gone. For no witch, young or old, can beat the flames of red and gold. Embers and ash will place the Odells firmly in the past." A tear slipped from the corner of my eye and traveled down my cheek. It left my jawline before I even thought to wipe it away. "Does that mean I'm going to die?"

Cooper jumped on top of the open book. "No! No! You know how this thing works. It's a riddle. It doesn't mean you're going to die." He stepped off the book and examined it carefully. "It's probably talking about the house. You know, it burning down, not you dying. That's crazy talk."

"I don't know." I leaned forward and wiped my nose. He flew across the room and landed on all fours. "Oh, sorry."

His body shook. "I hate it when you do that."

"I said sorry."

He hopped back onto the table and flipped the page in the book. "Read this one."

I read the passage out loud. "When it's time, the young witch will shine. To overcome the flames, she must put out the fire."

"See?" He popped onto my shoulder and nuzzled his furry brown face into the crook of my neck.

I squinted at the screen, reading the words to myself again. "I don't understand."

"The book's got psychological issues."

I rolled my eyes. "I'm serious."

"Okay, okay. Sometimes the book doesn't tell you what's going to happen, or give you a spell to fix what you need to fix. Sometimes it tells you what can happen. What's possible."

"So you're saying I still have a chance to fix this?"

He nodded, his little ears perky and expanded. "Did you hear that?"

I froze. "What?" I asked, barely above a whisper.

"That sound. That's what you call positivity."

I rolled my eyes. "I'd like to stay positive, but I kind of need a game plan."

And so we stayed up until sunrise creating just that.

～

Stella beat me to The Enchanted the next morning, which wasn't the norm, but I was tired, and that hour of sleep was desperately needed to implement the plan. She and Ryland sat across from each other outside at the small blue and purple mosaic-tiled table.

Ryland smiled at me, but his eyes returned to their original focus, my best friend. I understood. Stella's petite, fit figure garnered attention from passersby all the time, and when someone got a look at her dark blue eyes, they normally walked away with drool dripping from their mouths.

Stella had that "it" factor, that something not quite definable but appealing. I, on the other hand, could have starred in a B-rate movie as a female giant. I loved my height. I carried weight well because of it, but unlike Stella, I found it harder to get dates. The average male is five foot seven. I'm a smidgen under six feet, and I'd prefer not to look down on a date, so my options are limited.

I wasn't entirely comfortable with Ryland hitting on my best friend, but it might help me learn more about him.

Cooper roamed into The Enchanted and did a complete walk-through of each aisle. He examined the bookshelves, and since I'd learned he could read, I thought he might be looking for something that could help. More likely he was looking for a quiet place to nap, his favorite pastime other than eating tuna.

Cooper loved to sneak naps behind the spell books, which I'd never given a second thought to until he started using human words. The cat knew his spells, and several times this year he'd provided me with quick fixes to problems.

And people think cats are self-centered.

Mr. Charming flew over from the corner shelving unit at the far end of the store. I did a double-take. "Bessie, is that new?"

She looked up from the coffee pot and smiled at the bird condo. "You mean the perch? Sure is. Ryland brought it in this morning. Said his momma was a bird fan, and he'd made her one just like that in high school. Figured he'd whip one up for our store mascot."

I raised an eyebrow. "Whip it up? It's five levels and—" I walked toward it for a closer look. "Screwed together and stained."

She shrugged. "Don't shoot the messenger."

"Pretty bird. Pretty bird," Mr. Charming said.

I patted him on the head. "That you are, big guy."

He flew to Bessie and stood next to her while she cleaned the espresso machine. Mr. Charming always loved Bessie, and the more I saw them together, the more I understood their special connection. At some point I'd have to make a decision. I wanted him to be happy, and to be with the right person, and even though Bessie was like family, I wasn't quite ready to take the leap. All arrows pointed to their connection being magical, and ultimately, the universe would make the decision. Maybe it was just waiting for me to be ready.

"Bess." I sat at my table and opened my laptop. "Can we talk privately?"

She glanced around the empty store. "I don't think that will be a problem."

I eyed the two people flirting outside. "Come sit."

She scooted her chair close to mine. "What's up, buttercup?"

"I'm responsible for all of this, and I need to stop it before something else happens."

Her eyes widened as her jaw dropped. "No. You're not responsible for what happened."

"You don't understand." I'd taken photos of the book's pages, and I showed them to her now. "This is all about me." I told her about the photos and notes at the scene of both fires. "I feel so overwhelmed." She walked back to the counter, placed a raspberry scone on a plate, and set it beside my laptop. I broke off a piece and nibbled on it. "Thank you." I rubbed my temples. "I don't know what to do. I don't know who I can trust."

"You can trust me."

I smiled. "I know that. It's everyone else. I don't think I'm smart enough to handle this. I'm still a baby witch."

She laughed. "You are far from a baby."

"You know what I mean."

She nodded, then sat back down, grabbed my hand, and squeezed. "Abby, honey. You've grown a lot in the last year. Your mother passed, you learned you're a witch, and you handled a very intense situation. Not only are you one of the strongest people I know, you're one of the most powerful witches I've ever met."

"I don't feel very powerful, and I definitely don't feel like I know what to do with this power."

"Nobody does when it first comes to light, but you're growing stronger and smarter about it every day."

"But there's so much I don't know."

She laughed. "There's still so much I don't know too. That's always going to be the case. We may be witches, but the Universe didn't make us a whole lot different than humans. As we age, we become wiser, we learn to trust ourselves and our gifts. But Abby, we still need to trust our intuition. Just like humans, our intuition is what guides us. Follow it. It won't steer you wrong."

"Sometimes I can't figure out what my intuition is trying to tell me."

"That's normal. In time, it'll get easier." She crossed her arms over her chest. "Let me help you. That's why I'm here."

"I know," I said, cupping her hand in mine. "And I appreciate it, but right now, I've got to do it on my own. I can't explain it, but I feel strongly that if I don't do things a certain way, everything will just get worse."

A smile crept across her face. "That's your intuition talking."

I smiled too. "I guess it is." I bent my neck to the side. "There is one thing you can do for me."

"Of course."

"Watch your back. I've cast a protective spell on you, Stella, and Gabe, as well as the store, but just in case, you should do one too."

"Oh honey, nothing's going to hurt me."

"I don't want to take any chances. Whoever or whatever is doing this, they're serious."

"And what about you? You need protection too." She raised

her hand and then immediately dropped it as Austin Reynolds walked into the store.

He approached us and stood next to me, the unspoken words *I'm here to protect you* obvious in his stern jaw and thin, straight lips.

Bessie acknowledged the look, and I watched the concern on her face melt away. "Coffee?" she asked him.

"Yes, ma'am. I'd appreciate it. Black, if you don't mind."

"Not at all." She set up a fresh pot. I watched as she added a pinch of something that sent sparkles flying out of the grounds before switching the maker back to brew.

Austin sat across from me. "Gabe said you're aware of what I'm doing."

I nodded. "Stalking me." I wasn't entirely thrilled. It's one thing that humans don't see the magic in the world, but it's another having to explain my behavior. And my plan included some behaviors he might consider suspect.

Bessie set a large cup in front of him. He thanked her, then said to me, "Why don't you tell me about your connection to Doc? It might give me some clues about what's happening." He lifted the cup to his mouth, and several sparks flew from it.

His eyes followed the sparks, and then he set the cup back on the table without taking a sip.

Interesting.

The magical world consists of several different types of beings, and honestly, I'm not quite up to speed on all of them yet. Holiday Hills has a large population of shapeshifters, were-wolves, warlocks, and witches, but just the other day I learned my dry cleaners was owned by two time-traveling leprechauns. I didn't believe them until they told me dinosaurs weren't real. That one sent me straight to the internet, where I found a plethora of conspiracy theories about things I'd always consid-ered true. I know there are people who believe the world is flat, but I am confident it isn't. If that were true, Cooper and every other cat in the world would have already pushed most things off it. But the conspiracy theories about witches and other magical beings? Those I completely believed. How could I not? I wondered how many humans saw through the magical blockers to my world. There were exceptions to every rule, and I whole-heartedly believed some humans could see magic.

I just didn't think I knew any.

When I told Bessie about the dinosaurs, she couldn't stop laughing. "Never trust a leprechaun," she'd said.

No wonder my clothes always came back with stains.

Austin ran his hand through his thick black hair. He slowly rotated in his seat and stared at Stella and Ryland. "He's new to town, right?"

"Just like you." I didn't mean that to come out with such a bite to my tone.

He eyed me suspiciously. "You're not thrilled with our new relationship, are you?"

"I'm a big girl. I can take care of myself."

"Gabe explained what's going on, correct?"

I nodded, forcing my bottom lip to not stick out like a child who didn't get a piece of candy.

"Then you know this is important."

"Let's talk about that." I leaned toward him. "Someone is taking photos of me at random places and then proceeding to burn them down."

Cooper rubbed his head against my leg.

"While I understand the notes tell a different story, isn't it possible that I'm being used as a distraction? This is a small town, Deputy Chief Reynolds, and thanks to my late mother, everyone knows who I am."

"The photos aren't random, Abby. The notes prove that."

"I understand that, but that doesn't mean I'm not being used as a buffer to the truth."

He swirled the coffee around in the large cup but still didn't drink it. "Okay, I'm willing to consider that." Another swirl of the magical brew along with another glance at the sparkles floating from it. "Tell me the why."

"The why?"

"Every crime has a why. If you can figure out the reason, then it's often easy to find the criminal. So, what's the reason behind using you as a, what did you call it, buffer?"

"Like I said, people know me." I blushed at my growing ego. "For starters, I'm here every day, and I go for walks all the time, and the whole writing thing? It's kind of a mystery around here."

"What do you mean?"

"Everyone knows I write, and they all know my books are international best sellers, but only a few people know which ones they are." I crossed my legs. "I don't think I'm all that, but some people see me as a celebrity of sorts." Ugh. I sank down in my chair. I sounded like a prissy high school girl pretending to be humble. I am human, though. Okay, I'm not human, but I've spent ninety-nine percent of my life thinking and feeling human, and I still behave human a lot of the time. I just couldn't explain to him that about a year ago I learned about my witchy ways and solved a big murder case, and that magicals in town knew I was powerful. He'd just have to think I was stuck up.

"Okay, it's possible this has something to do with your writing. Maybe a competitive author, an editor who wants to be a famous author, something like that?"

I shook my head. "I can't think of anyone who would reach that level of crazy because of me or my books."

"What about Bessie?"

I narrowed my eyes. "What about Bessie?"

He angled his head toward her. "She owns a bookstore, which, by the way, I'm told has the best coffee in town. And am I correct in thinking she was your mom's best friend, too?"

He was new in town, so to know that, he'd have had to either ask around or overhear someone talking about it. "Yes, but what does that have to do with this?"

"Maybe she's jealous? Maybe she wants to be a writer, or maybe she wants some attention from you? Maybe your writing is getting in the way of your relationship?"

"You can't be serious."

"People don't surprise me."

Because based on what I'd learned over the last year, I was a powerful witch, and magicals wanted that. "This is a small town. It could be anyone, including my best friend out there, but it's not Bessie. I just know it." I pointed to Stella, who was patting Ryland's hand. She looked mesmerized by him, too.

"You've been targeted for a reason. You know what happened to Ronald Reagan, right?"

What did the former president have to do with me? "I'm sorry?"

"The assassination attempt. You know why Hinkley did that, right?"

"He thought if he killed Reagan, Jodie Foster would want him."

"It's possible someone is doing this for the same reason?"

"You can't seriously think someone is setting fires to impress me."

"It wouldn't be the first time, and it won't be the last."

Before I could respond, Stella marched in, her eyes sparkling and her cheeks flushed. "Abs, I need you. Stat!" She yanked on my arm and lifted me from my seat.

I wide-eyed the deputy chief. "Excuse me for a sec." I pulled my arm out of her grasp. "Stella! Seriously!"

A smile crept across his face as she dragged me behind a bookshelf.

Stella ignored my tone. "I think I'm in love!"

I rubbed the spot where she grabbed me. I'd have a bruise

later for sure. "You did not seriously just yank me from a conversation with the new deputy chief of police for this!"

The excited glint in her eye disappeared. "I'm sorry. I...I didn't realize it was such a big deal."

"It was! It is!" I toned down my volume. "We were talking about the fires. Regardless, that was totally rude."

Her shoulders sank. "You're right. It was. I apologize."

I took a deep breath and released it. "It's okay. Just in the future, please try not to drag me around like you're a caveman. It looks stupid considering I'm almost a foot taller than you." I smiled. "And it's kind of embarrassing." I felt bad for yelling at her. She was obviously excited, and I was being a little too intense. Okay, maybe I overreacted, but sometimes she needed boundaries.

She giggled. "I'm small and mighty."

"Yes, that you are. Now tell me why the big drag."

"We're going out. He asked me out."

I raised my hands and whispered toward the ceiling, "Hallelujah! Stella has a date!"

"I need you to come by and help me pick out something to wear."

"Take a breath, and yes, I can come by, but I don't need to. You should wear that black fitted top, the one with the heart-shaped neckline, and your black-and-white pinstriped skirt. You look amazing in that."

She managed to tone down the hyperventilating, and her face returned to its normal color. "You sure?"

I nodded. "While I'm all for you dating, please be careful, okay?"

Her smile faded. "You're really worried about these fires, aren't you?"

"I am." I didn't bother going into all the gory details. She was happy, and I was happy for her. I didn't need to screw with that, and I didn't want to worry her any more than I had to. I'd already cast a protective spell over her, so I hoped that would be enough.

She walked me back to my seat and apologized to Austin.

He nodded. "No harm, no foul."

She hitched her head toward me. "Tell that to Miss Uptight here."

I nudged her shoulder with mine. "Rude."

She smiled, then gave me a quick hug. "I'm trusting your outfit choice. I'll call you tomorrow."

"You'd better."

We watched as she sashayed out the door without a care in the world. I'd give anything to feel that way again.

"She's a trip," Austin said.

"She's got a date tonight with Ryland. She's a little excited."

"Really? I couldn't tell."

I smiled, but it quickly flipped upside down. "I hope he's for real."

"Do you have any reason to think otherwise?"

I shook my head. "But I don't have any reason to think he is, either. You know what I mean?"

"You sound as distrusting as a seasoned law enforcement officer."

"I've got good reason."

He nodded. "You want me to look into him?"

"You can do that?" I could too, but if Ryland was a magical, and he was responsible for the fires or notes, he could easily hide his true self from me. Shifters and werewolves couldn't, but that didn't mean they didn't have witch or warlock friends helping them.

He nodded. "And I will."

My shoulders relaxed. "Thank you. I'd appreciate that."

"It's my job." He swirled his coffee again.

I stared at it and finally said, "Are you going to drink that?"

He eyed the coffee in his cup. "Uh, I guess I'm not."

Interesting.

The way Austin's eyes darkened when he glanced at the coffee and then back at me had me wondering. He had a secret. I'm no psychic, but my intuition sent alarms buzzing in the pit of my stomach. Trust your gut, Abby. Sure, everyone had a secret, but in the magical world, they were more dangerous than I'd ever imagined.

CHAPTER 6

J used to consider myself patient, but having a bodyguard shot that thought out the window faster than Superman racing a speeding train. Austin's constant watchful eye made me claustrophobic. Besides, I had work to do, and it was harder to whip up magic while under a watchful eye. Especially an eye I wasn't sure wasn't magical itself. I hadn't noticed any magical tendencies other than him watching the sparkles leave his coffee, but that was enough for me to remain on guard around him. Desperate times called for desperate actions, and though I'd made a promise not to use magic just because I could, I had to break that.

I froze him. And it was pretty cool, too. Except it only lasted a second.

Austin shook his head and stretched his neck. A slight pop startled Cooper from his nap on the table. He jumped up onto all fours and hissed.

"Wow, back off there, little one," Austin said, then glanced at me. "That's weird."

"What?" His eyes drilled into mine, and I shifted in my seat. Tiny beads of sweat formed on my temples. He raised an eyebrow, then went back to reading a book about the Salem witch trials.

Bessie had over a thousand books in the store, and Austin picked the one about witches being burned on stakes. Coincidence? Doubtful.

He flipped through the pages. "You believe in witches?"

He didn't need magic to freeze me. "Sure. I mean, a lot of people practice Wicca."

"I mean witches that cast spells and work magic. You know, the kind that fly around on a broomstick."

"Esmerelda is offended. She uses a Swiffer." I held back a smile.

"I'm sorry?"

"Do you know what I do?"

He flicked his head toward my computer. "You're a writer."

I nodded. "Do you know what I write?"

"Gabe mentioned mysteries?"

"They're called cozy mysteries. I write about a witch who uses her magic to solve crimes. Mostly murders, but she's caught a kidnapper and a bank robber too."

"What's cozy about murder?"

"The murder doesn't happen on the page."

"Hmm."

"They're very popular."

"I'm sure they are." He pressed his lips together. "What's a Swiffer?"

We stayed at The Enchanted for a few more hours while I worked to delete what my computer magically typed into my work in progress. I'd delete and write something only to watch it disappear and what I'd deleted reappear. No amount of nose scratching helped change the process either.

Esmerelda's story was the key, and if I could figure out how to alter it, I would be able to stop the fires and catch whoever was responsible for them.

I pounded on the delete key with such intensity it stuck. Bessie handed me a plastic knife, which I used to pop it back into place. I'd deleted ten thousand words I hadn't typed, but in the process of unjamming the key, those same words reappeared. "Beeswax!"

Austin glanced over his reading glasses. "Beeswax?" The side of his mouth curled up.

I snarled at him. "I'm...I can't get the story how I want it." I read the words as they appeared on my screen. "I've got to go." I slammed the MacBook closed and stuffed it in my bag, then grabbed the rest of my things and headed toward the door.

"Whoa, hold on, Abby."

I whipped around and pointed my finger at him. "You stay!"

He held out his hands. "I've got orders from my boss."

My blood pressure rose. "Fine." I charged out, my cat and a deputy chief of police on my tail, then jogged to the police department and demanded to see the chief.

The front desk officer eyed Austin from behind the glass partition.

"It's okay," he said, and the officer let us in.

Gabe's door was open. I charged in, ready to scream, as Austin closed the door behind us.

"Enough," I said, wiping my sweaty palms on my pants. "I can't focus with a bodyguard. Tell him to back off."

Gabe stared at me and then Austin, who just shrugged. "Abby," Gabe said. "This is for your own good."

"I'm not a child," I complained, though the stomping of my foot showed them otherwise. "I can take care of myself. I have a deadline, and a serious problem on my hands, and I can't have Mr. Big here following me around like a lovesick puppy."

I felt Austin's smirk burning a hole in my back. "Mr. Big?"

Gabe swallowed back a laugh. I knew the expression on his face well. Wide eyes, raised eyebrows, and a gulping sound. "Lovesick puppy?"

Would turning them both into toads be self-serving? And more importantly, did I even care? I balled my hands into fists and bounced them off the sides of my legs. "You don't understand. I can't fix this with him around."

Gabe's eyes turned serious. "It's not your job to fix things."

I stared at the envelope on his desk. "Is that the one with the notes?"

He nodded.

I took a deep breath. "I'm really sorry, Gabe, but you've forced me to do this." I made up a spell on the fly, and had I not been in the middle of a major hissy fit, I would have been impressed.

"Step aside and give me space, their concerns for me, simply erase."

Both men blinked.

Gabe stared at me. "Ms. Odell?"

Ms. Odell? "Gabe, I mean, Chief Ryder, I was just checking on the, uh, the fires. Any news?"

He glanced at Austin. "Not yet, but don't worry. We've got our guys on it."

"Do you think it has anything to do with me?"

Gabe's brow furrowed. "Is there a reason we should?"

I eyed the files on his desk, noting the envelope with the notes had disappeared. "Nope." I laughed uncomfortably. "I just, uh, I was just joking."

"Joking? Ms. Odell, we have a job to do, but thank you for stopping by."

I blinked. "Oh, yeah. I…uh, I'm sorry. I just wanted to find out about my mom's place."

"You mean your mother's former home?"

"Technically it was mine, too."

"And you sold it a while back, correct?"

"Yes, but still, it was my house once, and I'm concerned about it."

He smiled. "I understand, and I appreciate your concern. When we have any additional information we can share with the public, I'll be sure to do just that."

"Uh, yeah. Thanks, Ga—I mean Chief Ryder. I appreciate that."

I grimaced as Austin escorted me out of Gabe's office. I'd wanted to stop the nonsense, not make me and Gabe practically strangers, but that might be best. At least for the time being. I could look into things a heck of a lot better without Austin looming close by.

Cooper sat outside the police department's door, his judgmental look nothing compared to the expression Gabe just left burned onto my soul. I swooped my familiar into my arms and whispered, "Not now. I don't know how long the spell's going to last." I hurried ahead.

"Where are we going?"

"To my mom's house."

We jogged to the house without a police tail. I'd started off carrying the cat, but after about a third of a block, I plopped him on the ground and let him use his four legs instead of my two. Grateful, I caught my breath and stared at the charred remains, a flood of memories drowning my mind and heart.

"Why was running here part of the plan." Cooper collapsed onto the grass and rolled over onto his back. "I'm gonna need a minute here."

I sat next to him and waited, taking full advantage of the minute to let my heart rate return to normal.

"I thought the plan was to stop whoever was starting the fires, not sulk in front of the last one."

"I'm not sulking. I'm drawing it out."

"But you don't have a pencil and paper."

I fell backward and groaned. "Can you just be serious for once?"

"Dude."

"You just made my point." Two cars drove by. A black car with a government-issued tag and a red SUV of some kind. I knew nothing about cars, so I couldn't identify either of them. "I'm trying to draw out the person, or, I don't know, thing responsible for this. This is about me." I pointed at my chest. "Someone is taking pictures of me around town, so they're probably watching me as I speak." I sat comfortably with my legs stretched out in front of me, doing my best to act casual and chill. "So, the sooner they realize that I'm waiting, the sooner I can take them down."

"Oh, boy."

I cringed. "Did that come out with confidence?" I needed someone to believe I wasn't scared.

"Sort of."

"I'll take it."

We sat there for three hours. I texted Stella to remind her what to wear, and then responded to no less than sixty messages and photos about her date—how to act, how to eat, what she thought she should wear, and a bunch more. It made the time go by and kept me awake. It did not keep Cooper awake, but not even an earthquake could do that.

I'd forgotten to charge my computer, and I used the battery up quickly.

The red SUV drove by again. It slowed to nearly a stop, but the windows were too tinted for me to see who was driving.

I flicked Cooper to rouse him. "Wake up."

He lifted his head and squinted. "What?"

"That's the second time that thing's driven by."

He stretched in the downward doggie position, then squinted toward the SUV as it crawled past. "I can't see inside."

"Neither can I." I pretended to ignore it when it came back around a third time.

Cooper chose another angle. He sauntered toward the road and sat smack dab in the middle of it, so when the government car, not the SUV, returned, it had to stop.

I ran toward him, scooping him up and holding him close. I told him he was a crazy cat, but that I appreciated his efforts.

The man driving the car stepped out. It was Austin.

"Ms. Odell, right?"

"Uh, you can call me Abby." We'd practically had dinner, breakfast, and lunch together, after all. But he didn't remember any of that.

"Abby then. Why are you hanging out on the lawn of a burned-down house?"

"It's my deceased mother's old home."

"Oh." The sympathy in his eyes hit me in the feels. "I'm sorry for your loss."

"Thank you."

"Hey, it's getting late. I've been to that pizza place in town. It's pretty good. You hungry? I could go for another slice."

History repeated itself, only slightly differently this time. "Uh, I can't." I checked my watch. "I'm helping a friend get ready for a date," I lied.

He nodded. "Stella?"

I blinked. "Yes, you remember that?"

He tilted his head. "Remember what? I heard her talking about it this morning when I stopped by The Enchanted."

Sometimes spells changed things witches didn't intend on. "Oh, yeah. That's right. But yeah, I'm going to help her get ready in a bit." Considering she'd already left, I wasn't in any hurry.

"Understand. Rain check?"

Nope. "Sure. Rain check."

"Great." He stood there awkwardly for a moment, and then smiled at Cooper. "Take care of that little runaway."

"I will, Officer."

The red SUV didn't come back around, but I was more concerned about why Austin Reynolds would show up from out of nowhere at my mom's old house, why he'd mention The Enchanted, and, if we were strangers in his eyes, why he'd suggest we have dinner together.

"He's fishy."

I nodded to my cat. "How come I didn't catch that before?"

"You did, but he used his sexy ways to distract you."

I held him in front of me and stared into his eyes, trying not to laugh at him for attempting to wiggle out of my grasp. "Sexy ways?"

"When you're asleep I watch Lifetime, not Hallmark."

I bit my bottom lip. "We need to follow Reynolds."

"We aren't cops. We don't have the skills."

"You're a cat. That's practically a stalker. We've got this."

"I like you, that's why I stalk you."

"Uh, you've been my cat for ten years. You'd better."

"Plus, it's my job. Cats don't normally like anyone—or anything, for that matter. I like you, but I love Bessie. She gives me tuna all the time."

"We're going home."

"It's kind of late, and I'm tired. Carry me?"

I rolled my eyes, then rubbed my nose and repeated *there's no place like home* in my head. It was silly, and I was surprised it worked.

Cooper was in my arms as we popped into my family room. "Whoa, you're really getting good at this."

A breeze wisped past, sending my long hair floating off my back. "Shush." I set him down and tiptoed toward the kitchen. "The window's open again."

He trailed behind, then scooted ahead of me. "Let me."

I stepped back and let him take the lead.

Cooper stood on the sill and stuck his head out. "No one's out there. You need to get a baseball bat for these kinds of things."

"You sound like an Italian grandmother from New York."

"I don't like this, Ab. Someone's trying to mess with you."

"I think it's all smoke and mirrors. They're trying to scare me, but it won't work."

"It won't?"

I pushed my shoulders back. "Nope. I'm not going to be bullied by anyone."

"What about anything?"

"That too." I grabbed a notebook from my kitchen drawer, then pulled out a pencil and got to business. It was time I sat down and noted everything I could about what happened so I could figure out the why. Or, if I couldn't do that, at least try to put some of the puzzle pieces together. Once I had a better picture in my head, I could implement my plan. The plan to stop the person, or thing, doing this.

Granted, it wasn't much of a plan. In fact, the more I thought about it, the more I realized that *finding responsible party, then stopping responsible party* wasn't a plan at all. But it was the best we could come up with without all the information, so I got to work on that information and the elusive *why*.

Two fires. Two notes. Two new men in town. One's human status iffy. The other just smarmy and expressing interest in my bestie. Neither could fit through my window, but that didn't mean they couldn't get in my house. And since I couldn't see any damage and didn't notice anything missing the first time, I didn't think my suspect was human.

So if Ryland or Austin was involved, I'd bet my piggy bank they weren't human.

Cooper snuggled up next to me on the couch. "Here's what I don't get. If that Ryland dude wants you, you know, for whatever reason he wants you, why go through Stella? Nothing personal, but she's pretty hot, so maybe that isn't about you?"

"Did you just call me ugly?"

His eyes widened. "That's where you went with that?"

I nodded. "That's where any woman would go with that."

"I'm a feline. I don't use looks to define a person's attractiveness. I determine that based on their smell."

"Fine, do I smell ugly?"

"You have your moments."

I narrowed my eyes at him. "Rude."

"I'm just sayin', if he's coming after you, the route he's taking may stick like glue."

"Dear Goddess, you're a poet."

"And I didn't know it."

"Please stop."

He sighed. "You've got to loosen up."

"I'll loosen up and chill when I stop the person or thing responsible for doing this." I leaned back and tapped my pencil against my chin. "Maybe a location spell? What do you think?"

"Can you feed me first? I'm starving."

I ignored him and leaned forward, tapping the pencil against the pad.

"Hello? I put my life on the line for you. That deserves a can of the good stuff." He stood on the notepad. "You in there?"

I rubbed my nose and a can of tuna appeared next to him. "Please don't make the groaning sounds."

"Groaning sounds?"

"That thing you do. Mmm, umm, ahhh, mmm. It's disgusting."

"I don't do that."

"Yes, you do."

"I don't complain about your snoring."

"Because I don't snore."

"And I'm a dog."

I rolled my eyes.

Two hours later, I'd retraced my steps over the past two weeks and found a pattern.

"Wow, I'm predictable."

I mapped out where I'd been, what I'd done, and approximately what time I'd been to each place.

"Here," I said, pointing to the name of the pizza place on the list. "I saw Austin there, and the book told a similar story." I pointed to the words "Doc's office" and tapped my pencil on it a few times. "Do you remember me yelling at the SUV?"

"You mean when you embarrassed me in front of strangers?"

"Yes, then."

"Yeah, I do. Do me a favor, take us back there."

"It's late, and it's chilly. You really want to go now?"

"No, I mean take us back to the fire."

My eyes widened. "I can do that?"

He held up his front paws to suggest he didn't know. "I'm assuming you can, and it's worth a shot, right? Maybe we can see who was driving the SUV."

"We could also go back to earlier today when we saw the SUV at my mom's old house and see if it's the same person."

"Or you could try a revealing spell."

"You make it sound so simple."

"Seems like it is."

"Well, you're wrong. Spells aren't easy. There's that whole appreciation for the Universe, the thanking, the rhyming—it's very complicated."

"Whine. Whine. Whine. Just be like Nike."

"It's alarming, the things you know about human society."

"We'll dive into that one day, a long time from now."

"Right."

I pressed my lips together and thought up a revealing spell. "Powers that be, please help me. Who sits in red, show me their head."

We waited.

And waited.

Cooper sighed. "That was kind of subpar. Can't you think of something better?"

"You try and rhyme on the fly."

"You just called me a poet."

I held out my palm. "Then go for it."

He meowed, stretched back into downward kitty, and said, "Help this witch scratch her itch, show the sight by adjusting the light."

We waited again.

He shrugged. "I never claimed to be a warlock."

I smiled. "That was a good effort, though." I tucked my leg underneath me. "Show me who's driving the red SUV."

My TV powered on, and the SUV appeared on the screen. My jaw dropped as I stared at Cooper, then the TV.

"Nice," he said.

The image was blurry, but we could see the shape of a masculine face. It also appeared in black and white, which wasn't all that helpful.

I squinted. "I can tell it's a man, but that's about it. It's too blurry."

"We need to transport back in time. Maybe we can get a better look there."

I'd never tried to send myself back in time. Was it possible? "Guess there's only one way to find out." I closed my eyes and bent my neck back. "Powers that be, hear my rhyme. Take me back to a place in time. Grant me a peek into my flaming past, send me there with this spell I cast."

My family room disappeared, and in the blink of an eye I was screaming at the red SUV again, only this time I saw a blurred vision of the man driving. He had dark hair, and he aimed his finger at me, cocking it like he was shooting a gun. I read his lips: "Bang, bang."

I rubbed my nose.

"Oh holy, holy, holy—" I paced through my small apartment. "That was scary. I didn't see that before. Did he do it before? What if he didn't? What if he was back in time with me?" I glanced around the room, searching for Cooper. He didn't usually stay quiet this long. He wasn't anywhere. "Cooper!"

I searched my entire house but couldn't find him. I must have left him in the past. I had to go back. I repeated the spell, and landed at the same time the man in the car mouthed *bang, bang*. I grabbed Cooper from the ground and held him close as I took off running. I had an idea, and if I ran fast enough, I might see what I needed.

"Where are we going?"

"Hold on!" I yelled. I rubbed my nose as I ran past the fire trucks and tripped when I landed on my mom's old front yard. Cooper flew from my grip and landed on all fours, but I wasn't so lucky. I rolled toward him and grabbed him again, then hopped up and ran behind the neighbor's car.

"What the…you gotta stop or you'll get a tuna surprise."

I dropped him to the ground. "Watch the road."

Three houses up, the red SUV peeked into view. It drove slowly down Mom's old street, slowed even more at the house, and then took off.

"He's casing the place."

"Who? Who's in the car?"

"I think it's Ryland."

"That and a dime will get you nothing." He headed toward the road. "You can't stay here long. It can mess up the future. We've got to get back."

"What do you mean, mess up the future?"

"Have you never seen *Back to the Future*?"

I shrugged. "Is that the one with the car that time travels?"

"It wasn't just a car. It was a DeLorean time machine."

"That movie's a little before my time."

"The point is, when Marty went back in time, he changed the

future. You may think that's movie fiction, but it's the way time travel works. You can come back and view things, but you can't act upon them. You don't know what kind of damage that can do."

"Stopping the fires can't damage anything. It can only make things better."

"No, Ab, it won't. Think of everything else that happened that day. People had meetings, others had babies. People died. People met the loves of their lives. You go in and change something, and that creates a domino effect. You don't have the right to do that."

He was right. I didn't know what I didn't know, and I trusted my familiar to guide me in the right direction. "But answer this: will seeing Ryland in the SUV change things?"

"Not if he traveled back in time too."

"At the exact same time we did? Is that possible?"

He nodded. "Why wouldn't it be? If he's watching you, he knows what you're doing."

I groaned. "This is way over my head."

"That's what I'm here for." He meowed. "By the way, once we're back in real time, can we stop at the store and get one of those stuffed mice? My catnip's all dried out. Does nothing for me now, so I ripped the mouse into shreds. Don't be scared when you find it in your shower."

I held up my hand. "Wait."

The soft hum of an engine broke the silence.

"There!" I pointed to the opposite corner, just in view down the street. "He's coming back!"

"This isn't good, Abby. We need to go."

"No. I'm not going to do anything. I'm just going to watch."

"I don't think it's a good idea."

"Duly noted. Now come on!"

When the SUV stopped in front of my mother's house, Cooper and I hid behind the corner of the neighbor's house for a better view. Ryland Augustus climbed out of the SUV and walked toward the corner of the house. He didn't appear to notice us or recall our presence at all.

"I don't think this is new. I think this is what happened already, and the Ryland in the SUV isn't the one from the future."

"This is getting confusing."

I nodded. "He's got something in his hand."

Cooper stretched his tiny brown head. "It looks like a box. Like the one you put that other cat's tags in."

I blinked. I'd saved Callie's tags from her collar after she'd crossed over the Rainbow Bridge when I was ten. I kept the box in my bra drawer. "Have you been snooping in my bra drawer?"

He shrugged. "I get bored."

"I feel like I need a shower now."

He sniffed my leg. "You do."

I rolled my eyes. Seriously. The cat knew how to cross a line, and I think he actually enjoyed it. "Get closer. See if you can tell what he's doing."

"I can tell what he's doing from here. He's burying the box under the azalea bush."

I stared at Ryland from my safe distance. He'd crouched down, and when he finished burying the box, he stood and swiped the dirt from his hands, then scanned the area before jogging back to his SUV. He waited a second and then drove off. I eyed Cooper, whose bottom half had disappeared. "Whoa. You're becoming invisible."

He glanced at his front paws. "Where?"

I pointed to his missing bottom half.

He crooked his head, and his eyes popped. "Yikes. We're disappearing."

I glanced at my hands but only saw the ground below where they should be. "Holy cow!"

"The spell's fading. We need to get back to the present or we're going to disappear completely. Just like in the movie. That writer was a freaking genius!"

My heart raced as I tried to conjure up a return spell but got nowhere. I tried and tried, but nothing seemed to work. When the same black car we saw before pulled up and stopped in front of my mom's house, I panicked.

So did Cooper. "Ab, we gotta bolt!" His back was completely gone, leaving just a brown head babbling like a puppet without strings.

It freaked me out.

"Just a sec." I pointed my handless arm at the car, yelping when I noticed my forearm had disappeared. "Oh, boy." I tried to rub my nose, but I no longer had anything to touch it with. "This isn't good!"

Austin Reynolds got out of the car and checked the area, then darted to where Ryland buried the box. As he dug quickly into the dirt, I found myself urging him to move faster.

He retrieved the box, rushed back to the car, and drove off.

"Spell of time, reverse my rhyme. Take us back to current time!"

I was suddenly dizzy and weak, watching the space around us whip into a spinning funnel. It stopped quickly, and we landed with a thud on my couch.

Cooper pushed himself onto all fours, swaying back and forth before regaining his balance. He bent his little head and checked his entire body. "Thank you, Universe." He rubbed his head against my leg. "That was awesome."

My head throbbed and my heart pounded. "I think I'm going to be sick." I bolted to my bathroom.

Luckily I wasn't, but that didn't stop Coop from coming in and staring at me expectantly. Why did I end up with a familiar that acted like an 80s movie character?

A red light flashed through my bedroom window. I peeked through my blinds and saw the cruiser stop in front of The Enchanted. Gabe climbed out of the vehicle, and a second later, my buzzer rang. I'd had the buzzer installed when I added a new bolting lock on the apartment doors. The neighbors didn't mind, and considering what happened months ago, I thought it was a smart idea. It might not stop the magicals, but it could slow them down.

Since I didn't want him to know I'd been spying out my window, I asked who it was and let him in when he responded, "Police, ma'am."

Gabe had never once referred to me as "ma'am." I didn't like it.

I stood with my back against my apartment door. He removed his hat as he stepped into view. "Hey, what's going on?"

I glanced at my clock. Cooper and I had traveled back in time several hours ago, but it was past midnight. Why would Gabe stop by at such a late hour? And still in uniform, with his cop face clear as the starlit moon.

"Ms. Odell, there's been an incident, and I'd like to ask you some questions."

I waved my hand for him to come inside. "An incident? Is this about the fires?"

He stood behind my couch. "Ms. Frone was attacked this evening. She's at the hospital now."

My stomach flipped. "Bessie? Is she okay?"

"She's going to be fine." He eyed my apartment and then settled his stare on me. "Can you tell me where you were at approximately seven this evening?"

Back in time with my supernatural cat. "I was here, in my apartment."

He examined my place with a judgmental eye, like he'd never been inside. "Can anyone verify that?"

My cat, but you wouldn't be able to understand him. "What's going on?"

"Ms. Frone was attacked at approximately 7:25 p.m. this evening."

I rubbed the back of my neck. "Do you think I attacked Bessie? She's like family to me."

He watched me carefully. I strongly considered turning him into a bug and smashing him, but I knew his suspicion toward me was my own doing. I'd cast that spell. I just didn't realize it would have this kind of effect.

"Ms. Frone was semi-conscious when we found her lying in front of her store. Her first words to my officer led him to believe you were involved."

"Semi-conscious?" I shifted my head, caught a glimpse of my purse on the table, and darted toward it. "I…I need to see her." I attempted to push past Gabe, but he grabbed my arm.

"Not quite yet, Ms. Odell."

I froze. The tight, authoritative squeeze on my bicep shocked me. I'd grown used to a gentler, more affectionate hand from the man.

What had I done? I needed to figure out what was happening and return things to normal fast.

I jerked my arm away. "Chief Ryder, please. The last thing I would do is hurt Bessie." I hitched my purse over my shoulder. "Now if you'll excuse me, I'm going to see her. Feel free to come along. I'm sure we can straighten this out when we get there." I stormed through my door, and when I realized I couldn't shut it and lock him in there, I flipped around and glared at him. "I need to lock my door."

His expression almost made me laugh. A little shocked, a little confused, a little angry. I didn't care. Bessie was all the family I had left, and it'd be a cold day in Georgia before I let something hurt her.

Again.

CHAPTER 7

*B*essie smiled when I entered the small, all-white emergency room at Holiday Hills General, but it flipped upside down when Gabe walked in behind me.

"I told them you didn't do this," she said as I rushed over and hugged her. "I was asking for you, not accusing you."

I turned around and glared at my once almost significant other. "Did you hear her?"

He stood like a statue, his hands behind his back and his feet spread out in line with his hips. "Yes, ma'am."

My narrowed eyes didn't portray the level of anger brewing inside me. "Then maybe you should go and find who did this instead of wasting your time accusing me?"

He didn't budge. "My team is working on it, ma'am."

Bessie raised a brow at me.

I eyed her, then him, then finally said, "Oh, screw it." I rubbed my nose, and Gabe disappeared. I glanced back at Bessie and widened my eyes at her smirk. "Well, come on. Why would he even think I could hurt you?" I hugged her again. "Are you okay?" I stepped back and examined her closely. "Nothing broken? Nothing punctured?"

"Punctured? What do you think happened?"

"I don't know, that's why I'm asking if anything's punctured."

"Nothing's punctured. It was scary, but I'm okay."

"What happened?"

"I was locking up and someone came from behind and attacked me."

I felt my carotid artery pulsing rapidly. "How? Did you see them?"

She shook her head, her bottom lip trembling. "It happened so fast. One minute, I'm twisting the bolt on the lock, and the next minute someone's arm is around my neck." She raised her fingers to her neck and caressed it. "He told me to stop helping you or I'd pay."

My jaw dropped. "He? Did you recognize his voice?"

She shook her head.

"And you told the officer it was a man?"

She paused. "At first, no, but when things were clearer, yes."

Then why would Gabe accuse me? Did he think I played a part in it? "Bessie, tell me what you felt when this happened."

"I felt like I couldn't breathe."

"I'm sure, but that's not what I mean. What did you feel—" I glanced around the room. "Witchy-wise? Did you feel like the person was human?"

She let her eyes slowly close as she leaned her head back against the pillow on the raised bed. "I...I can't tell. But his voice was low, determined. Almost guttural, he was so intense."

"When he spoke, was his mouth close to your ear? Was he higher? Did you feel any hair? You know, did something longer brush against you?"

She shook her head and touched the spot above her left ear. "Here. I felt pressure here." She closed her eyes again. "And his voice came down, like he's taller than me."

That wasn't uncommon. Bessie needed a stool to reach things most people could on their tiptoes. "What about his scent? Was he wearing any cologne? Did he smell, I don't know, maybe musky like an animal?"

"You think it was a werewolf?"

"I don't want to rule anything out."

"What do you think he meant when he said to stop helping you?"

I exhaled, sighing along with it. "I don't know. It could be anything. Helping me with my magic?" I glanced around the small room, then walked over to the door and closed it. "Or the fires. Could someone have found out what we did for Doc?"

"It's possible."

"It's all connected, I know that. I'm trying to figure it out."

"What can I do to help?"

I shook my head. "Nothing. Whoever did this to you was trying to send me a message. I don't want you involved. I want you to stay safe."

"Honey, you put a protective spell over me, remember? Whatever's happening is bigger than you can handle. You need help."

"No, I need you to be safe. I'll make another spell, and you can do one too. Two's better than one, right? And I'll go see Mystie. She'll create a spell too. Three spells will keep you safe." Unless, of course, Mystie was involved. I wasn't sure who I could trust.

"Sweetie, look at you. You're exhausted. You need to go home and get some rest before you do anything. I'm safe. I'll be more careful, I promise."

Before I had a chance to argue, the doctor walked in.

"Mrs. Frone? I'm Doctor Andover." He reviewed something on his clipboard. "We got your X-rays back, and everything looks good. You'll probably have a sore throat for a few days, and it's going to bruise, but we didn't see any internal damage."

Oh, thank God. "So I can take her home?"

He glanced at the door. "The police chief is waiting outside. He'd like to talk to Mrs. Frone first."

"Sure, yeah. Of course."

Gabe walked back in. "Bessie, I'd like to ask you a few more questions about what happened."

Her jaw stiffened and she talked through clenched teeth. "I've already told the officer who found me everything I know."

He eyed me suspiciously, then redirected the suspicion back to Bessie. "Very well then." He nodded toward me. "I'll be talking with you again, Ms. Odell."

As he walked out, I mimicked his stiff posture and professional demeanor. "I'll be talking with you again, my butt."

Bessie chuckled. "That's one serious spell you cast."

I smirked. "I think I did it wrong."

"I think you're right."

I helped her get ready to leave, reviewed the paperwork and instructions with the nurse, and then drove her home.

Mr. Charming greeted us at her door.

"Oh dear, he must be hungry."

The green parrot hopped on his feet. "Mr. Charming needs love. Needs love."

I extended my arm and he climbed on, nuzzling my neck with his beak. "I'm sorry, little guy. You must have been worried."

He flew into the parlor and perched on his favorite chair. Bessie headed straight for the kitchen, retrieved some berries from the fridge, and placed them on her coffee table. "Here you go, sweetie."

He flew over and rubbed against her arm. "Love. Love. Mr. Charming. Love."

My heart hurt for the bird.

Bessie refused to let me help her, shoving me out the door with a warning. "Go find the person responsible for this before something worse happens."

I immediately went back home and opened my manuscript. So much for getting any sleep.

Esmerelda studied the woman's neck. The bruise line darkened from a reddish blue to a deep purple. She should have known, should have

been there in time. She'd been warned. He'd told the woman to stop
helping, but she hadn't, and now she was dead.

I slammed my laptop shut. "No!"

Cooper woke from his deep sleep and pounced up from his side of the couch. "What? What's going on?" His little brown head darted back and forth as he propped up on his hind legs and made karate chop motions with his front paws. "I got you covered, Abs."

"Cooper, I need you to watch over Bessie."

He dropped back onto all fours. "Bessie? No. I help you. She's got the bird."

"The bird isn't her familiar, and if she has one, it's not doing a very good job. Whoever's doing this gave me a warning tonight. He didn't plan to kill Bessie, but he's coming for her again, and I need you to protect her."

"Can't you cast another protection spell over her?"

"I don't think it'll be enough. Please." I leaned toward him. "I can't lose her."

"I know. I know." He patted my forearm with his little paw. "I'll go, but I'm not staying. I'll get the bird up to speed if I have to, or I'll pull some strings and get her a real familiar."

"You can do that?"

He nodded, then hopped off the couch and smiled. "She's got the good tuna, so this won't suck."

I smiled too. "I appreciate this."

He nodded. "Yeah, I know. Now come on." He waved his paw. "Do your thing."

"Keep Ryland Augustus away from her, okay?"

He nodded. I rubbed my nose, and he was gone.

∾

I changed into a fresh pair of black leggings and a black hoodie. If someone needed to stay out of sight, the best way to do that at night was to wear black.

I wasn't exactly sure what was going on or why, but I knew Ryland and Austin were involved. Ryland's voice matched the description Bessie gave me, so I needed to start with him. More than anything, though, I needed the why. And the only way to get that was by finding out if he was magical.

I transported myself to his small cottage on the outside of the town's main drag. Ryland lived the good life, having updated the Civil War-era home in the short time he'd been in town. The porch, once held up by small discolored columns, stood supported by updated square blocks on top of stacked stone. The old, dried-out cement front porch was replaced by stone and cement, and his once single front door doubled to French doors painted bright red. He'd done a great job, and I couldn't help but wonder if he'd had a little magical help.

I stood across the street, staring at the dark home. No signs of life from inside, but that didn't mean he wasn't sleeping or sitting in the dark contemplating ways to hurt me.

The box flashed through my mind's eye. He'd left it and Austin dug it up. What was in the thing, and did Ryland know Austin went back for it? Was the plan to leave it for Austin? If so, why? Couldn't he just hand it to him? The sly handshake always worked for drug dealers on TV, and the box was small, so that was possible.

The more I thought about it, the more I realized in the few days since Austin came to town, I hadn't seen the two interact. Was that on purpose? Austin didn't appear to know Ryland, but that could have been an act. Maybe they didn't want to clue me in that they knew each other? Or maybe they really had never met.

I crept toward the side of the house and walked into a prickly rose bush. I lost my balance and tripped over it, slamming my body into the hardiplank siding with a thunk. I quickly swiped under my nose, and the next thing I knew, I was on the other side of the house. Good thing, too, because Ryland's light flipped on, and the entire side of the house lit up like a football stadium. I tiptoed toward the back, looking inside the house where I could, then looped back around to the front porch and glanced in the closest window.

The entire place was completely empty. Not a single piece of furniture. No coffee pot. No dishes on the counter. No table. No paper towels. Nothing. Who lived like that? Someone who wasn't human, that's who.

He'd renovated the outside to make the home look lived in to passersby, but hadn't taken the time to do the inside? That didn't make sense, unless he could whip up a spell and furnish the place.

I snuck behind the house again, and a light switched on. As I stared into the kitchen, I now knew Ryland Augustus wasn't human. I just wasn't sure what type of creature was standing by the sink.

A werewolf, maybe, or a shifter. It was hard to tell. Hair covered his body, but his face looked more human than the rest of him. That wasn't the norm for werewolves, but shifters were a different story. They could shift in portions and to various degrees. If Ryland was a shifter, he could keep his face looking more human, though I didn't know why he'd do that. Maybe he just preferred his human face, or maybe he'd been in the process of shifting when he heard or sensed me outside and paused to look? I ducked down just in case.

I stared at him over the bottom edge of the window, my hands shaking and my teeth chattering. I couldn't move. I was mesmerized and afraid. I felt like I'd swallowed a rock and it was stuck in the pit of my stomach. When his red pupils lit up, I dropped to the ground.

Something too close for comfort hissed. The patio door opened. Hairy Ryland charged out, his fur-covered arms up, his fingers claws. His manly head disappeared into a lump of gray and black fur. He growled. Something slithered by my leg. I bit my lip and prayed I wouldn't scream.

I couldn't move for fear he'd hear. Werewolves and shapeshifters had wicked senses, and hearing was one of their strongest. I watched him stare out toward the yard, take a few steps in that direction, and stop.

I held my breath. Please, I thought. Please let me disappear. I did my best to will myself away, but I couldn't touch my nose. Couldn't take the risk of being heard, felt, or seen. But just thinking about what I wanted to happen didn't work for me. Sometimes I could do small things, like move a chair an inch, but transporting my body someplace else was too big a task without the nose rub.

The hissing started again, and Ryland's shoulders straightened. He jerked his hairy head toward the back of his yard, his ears stiffening. He didn't move, and I was close enough to hear his breathing, but like me, he was holding his breath.

Focused on something I couldn't see, hear, or feel.

A large wolf-like creature appeared from the wooded area behind the yard. The thing was massive, not just in height. It had muscles like Thor and a head twice the size of a sixteen-pound bowling ball. It sprinted from the trees at lightning speed, making angry hissing sounds from nightmares and horror movies. It stood next to Ryland, intimidating and forceful. Ryland backed up, drew back his clawed hands, and whipped them forward in a defensive move as the other thing towered over him, hissing and snarling.

I raised my finger toward my nose and quickly dropped it back. I wanted to disappear and stay safe, but I needed to be there. I needed to stay calm, to watch, to see if either of them won and figure out who and what the larger, scarier hairy thing was.

It only took a few seconds for it to overpower Ryland. It had him down on the grass, its claws scratching at Ryland's fur-covered body. I didn't want Ryland to die, not yet. First I needed to know what was happening, and what was in that box. Death didn't do anyone justice. There were better punishments. Ryland would get what the Universe meant for him, but not until I had my answers.

I swiped my finger under my nose. The bigger of the two hairy monsters flew halfway across the yard and landed on its back. Ryland rolled over onto his side and pushed himself up on all fours, quickly checking out his surroundings. Then he stood and ran toward the other thing.

"Son of a gun," I grunted under my breath. I rubbed my nose harder, and Ryland flew backward, landing on his back.

He yelled something in English, but I was too busy freaking out to understand his words. The other fur monster charged at him again.

I stood up, pushed through the prickly bushes, and screamed, "No!" I rubbed my nose and then waved my hands wide apart. "Cage them!" I yelled.

A loud boom erupted from the sky as two large metal cages dropped down to contain the beasts. They grabbed the metal bars and shook their cages, growling loudly.

I caught my breath and stepped closer to the cages.

Ryland growled at me and shook his cage harder. I backed away as it rocked on the ground.

The other hairy thing showed me a big set of pointy teeth. I stumbled as I backed farther away, then quickly rubbed my nose and disappeared.

~

I reappeared in my apartment and immediately poured myself a glass of cold water. I drank it, then splashed water from the faucet onto my face. My body temperature soared along with my heart rate.

I had no clue what I'd witnessed, and I didn't know what exactly happened to the two monsters, but I knew it wasn't permanent.

I opened my laptop to my manuscript and stared at the words on the screen.

Esmerelda darted toward the back of the yard, but she wasn't fast enough to stop the evil coming for her. She fell to the ground and rolled to the side.

Nope, nope, and nope. I pounded the delete button until two-thirds of the document disappeared. As it began coming back, I rubbed my nose and said, "What tries to deceive, do not return. Protect this story or let it burn."

I couldn't erase it all, but I felt confident I'd hit the pause button on the drama and bought myself some time, though not much. If I didn't figure out how to stop what was going on by the time those things were humanized again, they would come after me. They saw me, and they knew I'd caged them, and even though I didn't know what was going on, they didn't know that, and they'd be extra intent on ending everything their way.

"I hate this." I spoke out loud like someone could hear me.

When a pot in my kitchen crashed to the floor, I realized someone could.

I twitched my nose and darted to the kitchen. Breathless, I yanked the window down and slid down the front of my cabinet, then sat on the floor, hugging my legs to my chest.

～

"I don't know." I repeated it twice before the words sank into Cooper's stubborn brain.

He repeated back a shortened version of what I told him. "You sure it was Ryland?"

I rolled my eyes. "You're not helping."

Bessie poured me a fresh cup of coffee, then set the pot on the counter and sat across from me. "What's the book say now?"

I stared at the blank page. "The same thing it did before, except less. I was able to delete most of it with a spell, but I'm not sure what that means." I scrolled back through the pages and saw bits and pieces of paragraphs I didn't write. "When this is over, I'm going to have to trash it all and start over."

"No, you won't." She cupped my hand in hers, then smiled and turned the laptop toward her. After a second of staring at it like the master of technology she wasn't, she flipped it back at me.

I stared at it with my mouth hanging open. "How'd you do that?"

"Magic, my dear. Magic."

I scanned the document quickly. She'd removed the magically written things completely. Had I known she could do that, I would have asked her first. "How'd you do that?"

"It's only temporary, but at least you've got a bit of time to figure it out before it starts up again." She smiled. "Now go find these monsters and stop them."

I "yes, ma'am'd" her and closed up shop. I needed to get to Ryland Augustus's backyard before a magical noticed two wolf-like Bigfoots in cages.

I made it there in thirty milliseconds flat, but I was too late. The cages were open and Gabe stood in front of them, head tilted.

I kept my calm as I approached, doing my best to act innocent. "What's Ryland been doing, keeping lions?"

Gabe stared at me. "Neighbors called these in earlier this morning. Heard some screaming back here and saw the cages, but they were empty."

"Screaming?"

"Argument of some sort's my guess."

I knew the neighbors, and they weren't magicals, so they must have heard something different than growling. "What's Ryland say?"

"Ms. Odell, this is a police investigation. May I ask what you're doing here?"

I blinked. "I, uh, I had to...I wanted to talk to Ryland about something."

"Then I suggest you come back another time."

I dragged my incisor over my bottom lip. "Yes, sir."

As I turned to leave, Austin Reynolds stepped out of his black sedan. A chill ran down my spine. Part of me wished I hadn't convinced Cooper to watch over Bessie, but the other half was glad he listened. Even though he was supposed to protect me, I wanted to protect him. I couldn't help but think that other hairy thing was standing in front of me, but in human form.

Austin approached me like we were old friends. "Abby." He grabbed my arm and pulled me behind a tree. "What're you doing here? Wasn't last night warning enough?"

My eyes practically popped out of my head. "How did...were you...did you...I, uh..."

"Yes, that was me. I'm a magical, and I'm trying to protect you, but you've got to stop putting yourself in dangerous situations. I can't be in two places at once."

I shook my head. "Wait, is Ryland the one doing this?"

"It's more complicated than that."

Gabe walked toward us, and Austin dropped my arm, stiffening as he faced his boss. "Chief."

Gabe nodded, then gave me a thin-lipped, I-just-got-scoldedby-the-principal stare. "Ms. Odell, I thought you were leaving." It wasn't a question.

"I, uh, I had some questions for the deputy chief." I did not like this version of Gabe. This version needed a good kick in the behind, and I was this close to doing just that.

"You'll have to wait. We're in the middle of an investigation."

Austin interrupted. "I'll walk her to her car." He guided me gently toward the street. "You didn't drive here, did you?"

I cringed. "What are you?"

"I told you, I'm here to protect you."

"That doesn't answer my question. *What* are you? A...a... what? A werewolf? A shapeshifter?"

He hesitated. "Don't worry about me. Just watch yourself, and stop trying to handle this. I'm on it, and I'll make sure nothing happens to you." He waved his hands toward his head.

As he headed back toward Gabe, I whispered, "Wait."

He turned around.

"What did you take from my mother's house?"

He stared at me.

"Ryland left something, and you took it. What was it?"

"Something that could change everything."

He charged off so quickly back to Gabe, I didn't have time to ask what that meant.

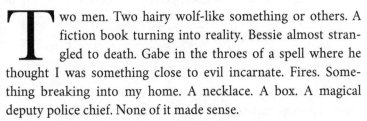

Two men. Two hairy wolf-like something or others. A fiction book turning into reality. Bessie almost strangled to death. Gabe in the throes of a spell where he thought I was something close to evil incarnate. Fires. Something breaking into my home. A necklace. A box. A magical deputy police chief. None of it made sense.

I jotted down more notes and drew a circle around Austin's name. I wrote *something that could change everything* in all caps and drew three lines under it. Austin was protecting me, but from what? What did the necklace and the box have to do with it all?

Unless the necklace was in the box, but if that was the case, if Austin was trying to protect me, he'd already have the necklace, wouldn't he? I knew less than I did before, but that wouldn't stop me from getting answers to my questions.

~

Cooper, Bessie, and Mr. Charming all greeted me at The Enchanted.

Cooper rubbed his head against my leg. "Got some tuna for me?"

"Mr. Charming loves you."

"No, and I love you too." I set my bag on my table.

Bessie offered me a cup of coffee, but I said no.

"It's almost ten o'clock. You're late today," she said.

"You shouldn't be working. You should be resting."

"Resting? I'm fine. Besides, if I stayed home, I'd just sit and worry. Working keeps my mind and body busy. I'll be too tired to worry when I'm home, and I'm too busy here to do it now." She swiped a cleaning towelette across the counter. "You didn't sleep after dropping me off, did you?"

"Sleep's overrated."

She raised an eyebrow. "What happened?"

"Nothing," I lied. "I just stopped by Ryland's house. Has he been here yet?"

She shook her head.

"What about Stella?"

"Nope."

"Okay, thanks." I headed back to the witchy section of the store. I'd used that section for years for my books, thinking it was just a bunch of fiction for wannabe witches. I laughed at the thought as I scanned the books, looking for anything that would help. I found three possible options and carried them to the counter. "I'll take these." I pulled out my debit card from the back of my phone case.

"They're yours."

"I can pay."

"Your money is no good here, silly. You know that."

I smiled. "Can you let me know if Stella or Ryland show up?"

"Of course."

"Thanks," I said, and headed out the door.

Cooper followed me. "I'm coming with you."

I crouched down and wiggled my finger at him. "No. I need you with Bessie. Please."

"This isn't how it works. I did you a favor before, and look what happened."

I twisted my mouth. "Wait, you—"

"Know you were almost eaten by two large hairy man-dogs? Yes."

"But how?"

"I have connections. Now you gonna carry me or make me walk."

I hiked him up near my shoulder.

"Thanks. I'm a bit tired today."

"You and me both."

We took my car instead of walking, and I drove to the potion store, or, as the humans viewed it, the herb and essential oils store. I mixed two powdered herbs along with one oil into a small bottle, closed it tightly with a dropper lid, and paid the sixty-two dollars it cost via debit card before driving to my mom's old house. I flipped through the pages of the first book I'd gotten from Bessie until I found what I needed. I followed the directions carefully.

Pick one wildflower or weed, preferably one of color, and place it in the desired location.

Done.

It then said to add two drops of the potion from six inches above the location, then wave my hands over it and repeat the spell. So I did.

"Wonders of life, magic, and sense, bring what was past to present tense."

As a writer, I admired the little play on words.

A small box appeared. I stared at it, then pulled off the lid.

Inside was a silver star hanging from a silver chain. I carefully removed it from the box, and as I closed my palm around it, a warming sensation seeped through my skin and deep into my soul. I opened my hand, and sparks flew from the necklace. I turned the star over and found an inscription.

The final piece for your true calling.

Then it disappeared, along with the box. The spell wasn't intended to return the necklace permanently, just long enough for me to see what it was.

And now I knew what Austin took. The question was, why didn't he give it to me?

CHAPTER 8

"Stella, it's me. Call me when you get this message."

It had been a while since I'd heard from her. She told me she'd planned a date with Ryland, but I saw him in his magical form, and Stella wasn't anywhere.

What had he done with her? I sent her several text messages and left three voicemails, but she didn't respond. Each text message said delivered but not read, so I knew she wasn't reading them.

I sped to her house, almost hitting her garage door as I skidded to a stop. I peeked into her garage through the window, but her car wasn't inside.

I called Bessie as I knocked on Stella's front door. "Is Stella there yet?"

"No. Abby, what's going on?"

"Call me if she shows up, okay?"

"Of course."

"And Bessie?"

"Yes, dear?"

"Please cast a protection spell over yourself."

"I already have."

"Thank you. I'll check in soon."

Cooper stared into Stella's window. "She's not there."

"Wait," I said, and rushed back to the car. I popped open my glove compartment and grabbed her spare house key, then sprinted back to the porch and unlocked her door. I stepped inside the kitchen quietly, hoping that if someone was there, they couldn't hear me.

I searched her entire house, but Cooper was right. She wasn't there. She hadn't been for a while, either. She'd made her bed, which she did every morning, and nothing seemed out of place. I checked her closet. The outfit I suggested she wear was missing. That sent chills up my spine.

I entered the spare room, which she used as an office, and opened her laptop. I knew her login info. It was easy. *Master Editor* was the name and *Your Book Needs Help* the password.

Stella had a sense of humor.

I checked her email. She hadn't opened anything since yesterday afternoon. That wasn't like Stella. I called her cell, and heard the familiar ringtone she'd picked for me from the other room. Stella never went anywhere without her phone. Never. I followed the loud horn sound and found her phone on the kitchen counter, behind her coffee pot. It was resting against the tile backsplash.

Stella would never purposely leave her phone, so either someone hid it from her or she left it there for me to find.

But why would she do that? Did she know she was in trouble? She hadn't answered any calls or texts in almost twenty-four hours, even texts from her father. That wasn't Stella. Something was up.

I couldn't call Gabe. He wouldn't understand, and he didn't like me all that much. I didn't feel comfortable calling Austin. He had the necklace and knew it was mine, but he didn't give it to me, so I didn't feel I could trust him. Besides, he hadn't been honest with me from the start, and I had a problem with that.

Not that I'd told him I was a magical, but he knew I was and should have been forthright with his magic.

I filled Cooper in on what happened that morning as we drove to Ryland's house. We knocked on the door, but no one answered.

I crooked my finger and headed around back. "Follow me."

The cages were gone, along with any signs they'd been there. No indentions in the grass, nothing.

I cupped my hand over my eyes and stared through the back window. The house was entirely different than before. I could see past the four-seat bar table into the main room. There was a gray sectional couch, a rustic wrought iron and wood coffee table, a flat-screen on the wall, and a comfy leather chair with an ottoman.

The photos on the wall gave it away, though—they looked too much like something you'd see in a model home to be personal choices. Had he not put anything on the walls, I would have fallen for it, but those were too impersonal to be hand-picked for taste. Which meant he'd made these things appear magically.

And that meant he wasn't a werewolf or a shapeshifter.

He was a warlock.

I tossed Cooper into the passenger seat of my car. He flew toward the door but stuck out his front paws to stop himself. "Where are we going?"

"To see Doc."

"Because?"

"Because I think there was something at his office that belonged to me." I stopped at a red light and waited forever for it to change.

"Can you be a little more specific, and while you're at it, try not to kill us?"

"I'm trying to save Stella and myself in the process."

"That's all good, but I mean with your driving."

I ignored him and sped through the green light. "Ryland isn't a shapeshifter or a werewolf. He's a warlock. You saw what he did to that place. And Austin. He's got the box, but if he's trying to protect me, why isn't he being honest with me?"

"What is this, a game of psychic Clue?"

"Feels that way, doesn't it?" I blinked. "Wait, you know about that game too?"

"I'll tell you my history someday. But for now, explain why you think there's something at Doc's."

"Think about it. There's a fire at my mom's old place, and we see Ryland bury something there. Then we see Austin dig it up and take it."

"And?"

"And we saw Ryland drive by the fire at Doc's. Maybe he left something there too. Maybe the fires are a distraction? It makes sense. Who's going to dig through a burned-out office searching for something?"

"Doc."

"I mean besides him. It makes sense."

"What if the necklace was hidden there, but that wasn't the best place for it, so Ryland burned down your mom's house and hid it there instead?"

I twisted my mouth. "True. There's only one way to find out, though, right?"

"There could still be smoldering ash there." He held up a paw. "I don't have shoes."

"I'll make sure your feet are safe. This is important. My gut tells me something else is there. Something that's necessary for whatever's supposed to happen. Like maybe the necklace has another piece, or another chain. I can't figure it out. I just know I have to check."

"So you think Austin's doing this?" He shook his head. "I'm confused."

"You and me both. I think one of them is trying to stop the other, but I'm not quite sure which. If Ryland has Stella, maybe he's the one coming for me. But that doesn't make sense because he's the one who left the necklace at the fire. Why would he do that?"

"You lost me about fifteen minutes ago. Give me the short version, 'kay?"

"I think Austin's doing this. It makes sense. He's new in town, in a big job where he can dictate what happens. He doesn't tell me he's a magical, but gets Gabe to assign him to me. And he found the box with the necklace and still hasn't said anything about it. Here's the thing. If he's got the box, why isn't this over? Why hasn't he killed me or whatever he's planning to do already?"

"You're going to tell me why, aren't you?"

"Because something's missing. And I'm pretty sure that something is hidden somewhere at Doc's. That's the only thing that makes sense."

"I take it back. This isn't Clue. This is a 3D puzzle and every piece is the same shape and color."

"Sounds about right."

When I performed the same spell at Doc's office that I did at my mom's house, I found a small box with a sterling silver broomstick charm and note. "Joined with the star, your true self will come, but watch where it lands, for danger looms near."

"I rhyme better than that, and I'm a cat."

I rolled my eyes.

"Who do you think wrote it?" he asked.

"I don't know. I don't recognize the writing."

We waited for the box to disappear, but it didn't. I glanced around the area, checking to see if anyone was watching, but I didn't see a soul anywhere. Holiday Hills wasn't a big town, but someone was always on the road during the day, or walking nearby. Except no one was around, and I wondered if that was on purpose. "Ryland must have left this here. That's why it's not disappearing, because it's still here in real time."

"If you say so."

"I need to find Ryland, and I definitely need to get that necklace from Austin." I stuffed the box into my pocket.

"How do you plan to do that?"

"I don't know just yet, but I'll figure it out."

"It's possible Austin's watching you. He could have been the one taking the photos before."

"Good. I hope he is. It'll be easier for me to beat him at his own game then."

His eyes widened. "If you say so."

"Listen, if he wants the charm, then he'll come for it. Same with Ryland. Right now I'm worried about Stella. I need to make sure she's okay, and once I've done that, I'll figure out what to do about the rest of this."

I drove back to my apartment and dug out my iPad and crystal, then searched for a map of the United States and placed my iPad flat on my coffee table. I hung the crystal over it and asked to find Ryland.

The crystal zeroed in on Holiday Hills. I enlarged the map to see the specific location, and it pointed to his house.

When I asked to find Stella, I got the same location.

Cooper tapped my leg with his paw. "Maybe they went dancing in Atlanta and stayed the night?"

"No, they were at Holiday Hills."

"Then don't ask me. I'm just a cat."

"I guess there's only one way to find out." I grabbed my purse, and we headed toward my car again.

Cooper stopped at the entrance to The Enchanted. "Wait. Bessie's got something in back that might help. Come on."

I followed him.

"Hey, what's the rush?" Bessie asked as we zipped past.

"Not sure," I said, my voice bouncing off the full bookshelves.

He went to the storage room and stood in front of a locked door. "Open it."

I rubbed my nose and opened the door magically. He galloped in, then stood by a wall of crystal-filled wands.

"What the…"

"Take that one." He pointed to the middle one with three yellow crystals down the front.

I yanked it from the wall, closed the door, and bolted back to the front of the store.

"That was quick," Bessie yelled. "That's my best wand. Be careful. It's powerful," she added before I slammed the door shut.

I climbed into the car and started it up. "Okay, what's this for?"

"Call it a power booster for your magic."

I kicked the car into drive and pressed my foot on the gas. I didn't let up until we made it to Ryland's. I parked three houses down, and just for safety, whipped up a minivan to cover my car. I didn't want anyone knowing I was there.

I knocked on the door but of course got no answer, so I rubbed my nose, and we appeared in the impersonal living room.

"What now?" Cooper asked.

Funny, I was wondering the same thing. "We check everything. If he's got Stella locked up here somewhere, we'll find her." I waved the wand through the air but it wasn't helping.

"If Austin's the one doing this, wouldn't he have her?"

"Yes. No. I don't know. All I know is she was supposed to go on a date with Ryland, and I haven't heard from her since."

"Maybe you need to call the police?"

"Right, because Austin's a cop, and he's been so helpful. No." I stomped my foot. "I don't trust anyone. Ryland's got Stella somewhere, and I'm going to get her."

"Then what?"

"I'll send him off to a faraway island, that's what."

"Alrighty then. Let's get our search going."

We did just that. We checked under the bed, in the closets, in the kitchen pantry and cabinets, and even in the creepy, dusty cellar.

I wasn't a fan of dark, damp places, but Cooper had a field day. He found a mouse nest. When he showed me, I screamed and bolted upright from my crouched position, smacking my head on the ceiling. After a minute, the dizziness passed.

"Sorry about that."

"I prefer the cloth mice," I said, shuddering at the thought of the real ones.

"I'm partial to both."

I stomped away and continued my search. Five minutes later, I sat on his uncomfortable dark leather couch and held my head in my hands. "There's nothing. I don't understand. Not even a sign of them here."

Footsteps hit the ceiling. I crouched down and lifted my finger to my mouth. "Did you hear that?"

Cooper nodded. The mice scurried in several directions. I scooted over a few feet for fear one would crawl up my pants.

The steps continued. Thump. Thump. Slam. Thump. Thump. Slam.

Whoever was up there was looking for something too. I held Cooper close to my chest, the wand stuffed in my armpit, until the stomping stopped. We waited a little longer and then crept up the ladder into the laundry room. Cooper peeked out and gave the all clear.

I rushed to the window and watched the back end of a familiar car turning off the street with Austin Reynolds in the driver's seat. "It's Austin. He's either looking for Ryland or me."

"But Ryland's not here."

"No, I think he is, and he's hiding."

"I think none of this makes sense."

"But it does. We've just been looking at it all wrong."

"Please, show me the right way to look at it, then, because I'm more confused than after an extra-long sniff of the kitty pot."

"I sort of already did, but here it is again. Austin's the one doing all this. He's probably not even a real cop. It's probably magic. He came after Ryland, remember?"

"And told you about it. And wasn't it Ryland you saw all haired up first?"

I nodded. "Maybe he was expecting Austin? A good warlock would, right?"

He shrugged. "I guess."

"So what if Ryland hid the necklace and charm from Austin? But then Austin finds the necklace, which, like I said before, he's still got. Austin shows up at Ryland's to get the charm, but Ryland's expecting him, so he gets all wolfed out and they fight. I tossed them both in cages before one of them got hurt, and before Austin could get the charm."

"But what about Stella?"

"Stella went MIA the same night Bessie was almost killed."

"Didn't you say the voice she heard was low, like Ryland's?"

"Yeah, but that could be manipulated by magic. I think it was Austin, and when Ryland found out, he took Stella someplace safe."

"Because he was afraid Austin would come for her too?"

"Like Bessie was a warning for me."

He nodded. "I can get behind this."

I stepped into Ryland's kitchen and opened a random drawer. "They're here. We can't see them, but I can feel them. I know they're here." I tilted my head back. "Can you smell that?"

He jumped on the counter and stuck out his head, then meowed. "That's the perfume she wears, isn't it?" He shook his head. "It's citrusy. Cats hate that smell."

"Right. It's Stella's perfume. They're here."

"So whip up a spell and find them."

I wandered around the house, following the faint scent of her perfume. Could they be hiding in some alternative version of time? Some different universe? Were they invisible? And how the heck was he keeping it all from Stella?

A car engine roared nearby. I ducked and stuck my head around the corner of the window to watch the black sedan zip past again.

Cooper rubbed against my leg. "He knows we're here."

I crawled back to the kitchen just in case he came around again and pressed my back into the counter. "Of earth and light, and day and night, show me what is not in sight." I rubbed the heck out of my nose and waved the wand in the air.

The wand disappeared, but the spell worked. I had no idea what happened to the wand, but something made me feel like it returned to its place on the wall.

Stella's petite body shimmered into view. Soon after, Ryland appeared. Stella was munching on a bowl of chips while Ryland prepared something on the stove. It was like watching a movie. They chatted about Holiday Hills and then the subject changed to me.

"I think that new deputy chief has the hots for your best friend," Ryland said.

Stella smiled. "You think? She's all but hooked up with Gabe, though, and she's crushed on him for a long time. I don't think the new guy has a shot."

Ryland stirred something in the pot on the stove. "I hope not." He turned around and stared directly down at me. "He doesn't have her best interests in mind."

I blinked and pointed to myself. Ryland looked straight at me and nodded.

He could see me! He knew I was there!

"What do you mean?" Stella asked.

I eyed her carefully, then stood and walked over to her, waving my hand in her face.

Nothing. She didn't have a clue I was there.

"It means I don't trust the guy."

"He's a cop. What's not to trust?"

"The world is full of dirty cops. I don't know what it is, but there's something off about him. If I were your friend, I'd stay clear of him. He'll show his true colors soon enough."

"What about you?" Stella's tone was light, flirty. "When are you going to show your true colors?"

He smiled at her, then me. "I think having you here and not trying any funny stuff shows them just fine."

I was right, he was protecting her.

From Austin.

They disappeared, and I rushed to find Cooper, who'd unfortunately gone back to the cellar and was in the middle of a cat and mouse thing.

He dropped the mouse from his mouth when he saw me staring at him. "What? I'm not hurting him."

"I was right. It's Austin."

"Did you find Stella?"

"Sort of. They're here. I cast the spell like you suggested, and it showed me an alternate universe or something. Ryland saw me, and he gave me a message."

"What'd he say?"

"That I can't trust Austin."

Which meant he was the one who hurt Bessie, and if he wanted the charm, he'd do what he had to in order to get it.

～

"I need to see Chief Reynolds, please."

"He's in a meeting. You'll have to wait." The front desk clerk pointed to the chairs lining the entryway.

I sat and waited. An hour later, I knocked on the glass again. "This is very important."

"He's still in a meeting, ma'am. Perhaps you could make an appointment?"

"No, that's okay." I walked out and stood in front of his police cruiser. "I hate to do this, but I don't have any other choice." I rubbed my nose, and the cruiser's front window exploded. I dropped to the ground and held my head under my arms, wishing I could cover my ears as the sirens blared next to me.

The doors to the station burst open, and Austin and Gabe rushed out, guns drawn.

I pointed toward the parking lot exit. "That way!" I screamed. "Kid dressed in a black hoodie!"

Gabe took off running, but Austin stayed. He crouched down and helped me stand. His touch was gentle but commanding. If I didn't know better, I'd swear he was being genuine, but I did know better, and I didn't trust him.

Wrong guy, I screamed in my head. I needed Gabe to stay. Time to improvise. "Go! There were two, I think! One ran that way!" I pointed toward the other end of the lot.

Austin eyed me suspiciously, then took off running. Another officer rushed out from the building, clicked something, and turned off the alarm.

I pointed at Austin's back. "That way!"

He took off running.

I slid my finger under my nose. "Gabe, here!"

Gabe appeared a few feet away and walked toward me.

"Did you catch them?" I hoped my shaky voice didn't betray my fib.

"No, ma'am. I didn't see anyone. Why don't you come inside and tell me what happened?"

Bingo! He fell for it. We walked into his office, and he closed the door. "Have a seat."

I sat.

"Tell me what happened, please."

"Yes, sir, but first. Powers that be, reverse the spell, bring back the man who knew me sort of well." I rubbed my nose and waited.

Gabe touched my arm. "Are you okay?"

The softness in his touch sent good shivers down my spine. "Oh, how I've missed you."

He laughed. "I've missed you too. Once we figure out who's setting these fires we'll get back to normal." He brushed his hand over my shoulder. "Or maybe something better."

"Gabe, I need to tell you something, and I'm not sure how to say it, but I need you to listen to me, okay? And trust me. You definitely need to trust me."

He furrowed his brow. "What's going on?" He leaned against the side of his desk and crossed his arms.

"Something's not right with Austin. I don't think he should be your deputy chief."

He raised an eyebrow. "Abby, he comes highly recommended, and he's doing great things in the department already."

"I think he's trying to hurt me."

His eyes widened but he stayed calm. "Why do you say that?"

"I...I..." I twisted my hands into a knot on my lap. "Can you sit? It's awkward with you standing."

He sat on the other side of his desk and leaned forward in anticipation. "Better?"

I nodded and said quickly, all in one long breath, "I'm going to tell you this because I don't know what else to do, and then I'm going to have to cast a spell on you afterward so you don't remember any of it. I don't know if it'll work, or if I'll end up in some kind of magical prison or whatever, but here it goes." I took a deep breath and exhaled. "I'm a witch."

He stared at me.

And stared at me.

I realized I hadn't taken a breath since I told him the truth. I inhaled and released it. "And Austin is trying to do something. Something that will stop me from, I don't know, being whole or…" I waved my hand away from my face. "I know it's ridiculous, but please, you have to believe me."

"Did you hit your head on the blacktop? Should I call an ambulance?"

"No, please, just listen. I'm fine. It's Austin, he's the one starting the fires."

"You're a witch?" He shook his head. "I'm sorry. I'm not sure what you're saying."

"Look, you don't have to believe in witches, but I need you to believe in me. I haven't given you any reason not to."

He leaned back and relaxed his shoulders. "I have a cousin who practices Wicca. Is that what you mean?"

"No, Gabe. I'm not practicing Wicca. I'm an honest to goodness witch. Like, one that has magical powers. All I have to do is rub my nose and stuff happens."

He pressed his lips together. "Are you sure you didn't hit your head?"

"Okay, watch." I rubbed under my nose and his laptop slammed shut. "See?"

He stared at his desk. "See what?"

"Your laptop. I shut it with magic."

He eyed the laptop and then me. "Abby, it's still open."

Crap! He couldn't see my magic because humans weren't capable of seeing it. "Okay, wait. Let me think." I mumbled under my breath, "I need your help. I know this is wrong, but show this man where he doesn't belong."

Sparkles floated around the room, but then everything was the same as before. I eyed Gabe carefully, but if he saw the sparkles, I couldn't tell.

"Okay, watch now." I rubbed my nose again, and the laptop slammed shut.

Gabe stared at it and pushed his chair back from the desk. He glanced up at me, then at the computer, then at me again.

I rubbed under my nose and opened the laptop once more.

Gabe jumped from his seat. "What's going on?"

The confusion and fear bleeding from his pores made me instantly regret my decision. Thankfully, it was temporary. I'd figure out how to erase it all from his memory, and hopefully I wouldn't be reprimanded for using magic for personal gain. I would argue that point to the death because the lives of the people I cared about were more than personal gain for me. They were vital to the community and the people who loved them. "Gabe, there is a whole world of magic you can't see. I know it's crazy, but it's real. You have to believe me."

His eyes stayed the size of Coke bottle bottoms, but other than that, he'd gathered his composure and steadied his shaking shoulders. He rubbed his lips together and swallowed. I watched his Adam's apple bounce up and down. I'd just started getting to know Gabe. We'd only been spending time together for a few months, and it took most of that for him to even begin coming out of his shell. Losing his wife was the hardest thing he'd gone through, and he made that perfectly clear. He wanted slow and steady—his words—and he worried if he opened his heart to someone else, it would break again.

And I might have just done that, but I didn't want to be that person. I wanted to be the one who helped him heal, helped him understand love again. Telling him I was a witch likely tossed all of that right out the window, but I couldn't backtrack. Too many things were at stake, and I needed him to understand.

"How is this possible?"

I took a deep breath before telling him the short version of my story. "We don't have much time, but I need you to listen carefully, and trust me. Can you do that?"

He nodded.

"Holiday Hills is a magical town. There are several people here you may think are your everyday run-of-the-mill humans, but they're not. Bessie, for example, is a witch. The woman at the bakery, Mrs. Clementine? She's a witch." I didn't mention the shapeshifters or the werewolves because who'd actually believe that? I still struggled with it sometimes. "When magic happens, humans can't see it. You see something else." I shook my head. "I know I'm not making sense, and I know it sounds crazy, but I can prove it."

He raised an eyebrow. "I already saw my computer open and close itself, and I'm not a witch."

It would be warlock, but I didn't bother correcting him. "Exactly, because I let you, but if you called someone else in, they wouldn't see it."

He hit a button on his phone. "Can you come into my office for a moment?"

The front desk officer stepped in. "Yes, sir?"

Gabe eyed me. I rubbed my nose and his pencil holder fell onto the floor. He watched the officer, but nothing happened. The officer didn't blink, move away, or anything. He just stood there waiting for Gabe to say something. I rubbed my nose again and let the small metal cup fill back up with the scattered pencils and then hover in front of the man's face. If I weren't so desperate, I'd laugh. I placed it gently on the desk again, then watched Gabe blink.

"Has Deputy Chief Reynolds returned?" Gabe asked.

"No, sir. Should I send him in when he does?"

"Get on the radio and tell him to do a drive through town. Ms. Odell here says there were two teenagers setting off car alarms. Have him continue to look for them, please."

"Yes, sir." He nodded and then left the office.

I stared at him, tapping my foot on the floor and waiting for him to say something.

"I don't know what to say. I don't know what's going on, but I'm going to trust you." He leaned back, though I wasn't sure he was as relaxed as he wanted me to believe. "Start from the beginning."

And I did. I told him every confusing detail, how I saw bits and pieces of things, how none of it made a whole lot of sense, how Ryland was somehow involved but I wasn't sure exactly how, though I thought he was one of the good guys. And most importantly, I said that Austin wasn't good, and I needed to get the necklace from him before someone got hurt. To validate and prove my points, I pulled the charm from my pocket and showed it to him. "I don't know what it all means, and the only way I'll find out is by joining this and the star together on the chain."

"Why not just ask Austin what's going on?"

If only it were that simple. "He hasn't been honest with me. He's a magical, and usually magicals show themselves to other magicals."

"Usually?"

"That's a conversation for later. Just trust me. The only reason he wouldn't show me his true self is because he's up to something bad."

"You don't think it's possible he's hiding it because he's trying to help you?"

"No. I know that's not the case."

He stood and put on his official police chief hat. "Let's go."

I wiggled out of my seat. "Go where?"

"I'm the police chief. If this town is what you say, and if you want me to help you, I need a quick tour of the real Holiday Hills. I can't fight something I can't see."

Tears filled my eyes. "You believe me?"

He stepped closer, placed his hands on my shoulders, and smiled. "I've never met a woman who could move objects with her mind. Let's just say getting a beer while sitting on the couch watching football just got a whole lot easier."

He really knew how to make a girl feel good.

We took his car, and I gave him what I named the "magical tour of Holiday Hills." Since he had a bird's-eye view of the real town, it was like watching a baby at a park for the first time. He wanted to touch, smell, taste, hear, and see everything.

We started at The Enchanted.

"We don't have a lot of time. Austin's going to figure out I've told you."

"You let me handle Austin."

"I'm not sure you can."

Gabe smiled. "I promise you, I can."

Bessie poured him a cup of coffee, and Gabe smiled as the sparkles of light drifted from it.

"Interesting."

Bessie's eyes popped.

I shook my head slightly and touched my ear. She stared at me and then watched Gabe guzzle the hot drink.

"Bessie, the wand. I used it and then it disappeared. I feel like it came back here, but I don't know for sure."

"It did its job. It wouldn't have disappeared otherwise. Don't you worry about the wand, sweetie. It's probably back in the closet."

I breathed a sigh of relief. "Good." I hitched my head toward Gabe. "We should get going."

"In a minute." He smiled at Bessie. "I just want to take a look around the store."

As he walked away, Bessie grabbed my arm and yanked me behind the counter. "What in the beeswax is going on? Did you tell him?"

I cringed. "I had to. I need his help. Austin's doing this, and he's a magical, and I didn't know what else to do."

"There are rules, Abby. You're putting yourself in danger, not to mention you could lose your powers forever."

"I'm not doing this for myself, Bessie. I'm doing it to keep the people I care about safe."

"At what expense?"

"My own, and I'm good with that."

"That could mean the end of you."

I shivered at the thought. "I'm willing to take the risk if that means the people I care about won't get hurt." She didn't know Ryland was keeping Stella safe, and I wanted it to remain that way. Something told me the less she knew, the better off she was.

"Have you talked to Stella? I haven't seen her."

"She's fine," I said. "She's visiting her dad."

"It's probably better she's not here for this anyway. You could have inadvertently exposed her to magic too."

"Right."

Gabe walked over from the back of the store. "You've got a lot of great books here, Bessie. Can't believe I didn't notice before." He set two books on the counter, *The History of Magic* and *Modern Magic in Times of Change*. Then he placed two twenties on top of them.

"No," Bessie said. "Your money's no good here, Chief."

He pushed it toward her. "I insist."

She rang up his books and handed him the change and receipt.

We said our goodbyes, and as we left, the door opened for us. I assumed it was Bessie's doing until we got in Gabe's car.

That's when my entire life flipped upside down.

CHAPTER 9

*G*abe's department car was fairly new, and it had one of those push start engines. I'd watched him push it when we left the station, but when the car started without him touching the button, I gasped.

He shifted his head toward me and smiled. "I know this is a lot to take in, but…"

My jaw dropped to my lap.

The car kicked into reverse all by itself, and my entire body stiffened.

He saw the shock, or maybe fear, in my eyes, and his smile shifted. "No, Abby, it's not what you think."

I gripped the door handle. "I…I'm…" I couldn't speak. I couldn't think.

"I'm sorry you had to find out this way. I planned to tell you when the time was right, but that came a little sooner than I'd hoped."

"Tell me what? Are you a warlock?"

He nodded. "I'm a magical, Abby. Just like you."

I shook my head. "No. No, no, no! You can't be. You—no. Just no."

He turned the car out of the spot and drove up the street. "Yes, and I was sent here to guide you, to protect you."

To protect me? Like Austin? I didn't know what to think or believe. Gabe lied to me. He hid his magic from me. Why?

"I work for the MBI. We specialize in upholding the laws of magic, and I was assigned your case a few years ago."

"My case?"

He nodded. "We knew you'd be coming into your powers soon, and they sent me here to watch over you, to keep you safe, and at some point, maybe even bring you on board."

"Is this a joke?"

He drove toward the outskirts of town. "No. I know about Austin. That's why I hired him. I needed to draw him out so we could catch him."

"Esmerelda. She's—" She'd taken a fictional job with the Magical Bureau of Investigations. Things were hitting a little too close to home.

"A lot like you, yes. It's not a coincidence. For the most part, you've been writing your life, and when your book started writing itself, we realized what was coming and had to take action."

"No. It's fiction. I write fiction."

"You have, yes, but this recent book, it's fairly on point, wouldn't you say?"

I buried my head in my hands. I thought I'd shocked Gabe, but all along, he'd been lying to me. I looked up at him, tears streaming down my face. Thank God for waterproof mascara. "Why didn't you tell me?"

"For the same reason you didn't tell me. I'm not supposed to, but I can't lie to you anymore. You deserve to know the truth, and I should have been honest with you from the start."

"Am I right? Did Austin hurt Bessie? And Ryland, he works with you, doesn't he?"

He nodded. "He's undercover. And yes, Austin hurt Bessie,

and I'm sorry for that. If I'd have known that was coming, I would have stopped him."

"But you accused me. You've been acting like I am evil incarnate."

"Because you cast a spell to change how I saw you."

He was right, of course, but I couldn't help wondering what was real and what wasn't. "What about before? The things happening between us. Was that real?"

He placed his hand on my knee. "My feelings for you are real, Abby. I played along with your spell because I had to."

I stared out at the road. We'd reached the end of Holiday Hills. "Where are you taking me? We have to find Austin. I can't let him hurt anyone else."

"Austin's not going to hurt anyone right now. I promise you that."

We pulled into a large parking lot that circled around a massive, windowless black building. I'd been to this area many times, but never once saw this place. "Is this...what is this? I wrote about a place like this."

"I know. It's the MBI headquarters."

"How come I've never seen it before? I mean, outside of my imagination, that is."

He shut off the car. "You weren't allowed until now." He unlocked the doors. "Come on, we've got to get you caught up."

"Wait!"

"What?"

"Cooper! He was with me earlier, but he's gone. What if something's happened to him?"

"Your familiar is fine. He's inside."

My eyes widened. "He knows about you?"

"He does now. It took some convincing, but he's good to go."

I couldn't say the same for myself.

The inside of the MBI office was an exact replica of how I'd described it in my book. Sterile metal furniture, white walls, no colors at all. I wouldn't have been surprised if men in black suits and dark sunglasses gathered in the lobby.

As I judged everything around me with a stern eye, something rubbed against my leg. I jumped.

"Hey, chill out, will ya? I've already come close to a heart attack once today."

I bent down and scooped Cooper into my arms, cradling him close to my face. "You're okay! Thank God. I was worried about you."

He nibbled on my hair for a second, then spat it out of his mouth. "I hate that shampoo."

I had my cat back, and he hadn't changed at all.

He eyed Gabe. "Can you believe that guy? All this time and I didn't sniff out any magic around him. Either I'm off my game, or the dude's good."

"I think he's fooled a lot of people."

"We've got a lot to do. You ready for this?"

"Boy, they sure turned you over to the dark side, didn't they?"

"They hit me right in the feels. Three jumbo cans of Chicken of the Sea, and I was a goner."

I laughed. "I could use a Hershey Bar."

A metal table stacked two feet high with Hershey Bars appeared before us.

Cooper's silky little brick-like body went board still. "Whoa."

"If only they were calorie free."

"This place makes magic happen, not miracles." He nuzzled his little head into the crook of my neck. "You ready?"

I grabbed a chocolate bar from the table and set him down. "Where'd Gabe go?"

He pointed a paw toward a steel door. "Through there. Come on."

~

After forty-five minutes of straight babble from Ambrose Bellamy, a warlock and the head of the MBI, they carted me off to a small room with white walls, another metal table—minus the chocolate bars—and a cold metal chair. The short woman with flaming red hair who'd escorted me there said I could have water or Coke.

I chose water. She held out her hand and a blackberry Hint appeared. "Your favorite, correct?"

I needed a vacation already. All that babble was nothing more than a sales pitch for me to sign on the dotted line that would forever bind me to the MBI as an operative, and the more Ambrose rambled on about it, the sturdier I stood on the *no way, Jose* side of the fence.

Not happening. Nope, nope, and nope.

Gabe walked through the door, and Cooper followed behind him. "We have an issue."

"Are you sure you're not a shapeshifter?"

He smiled. "You know shifters can't make magic. Like I said, I'm a warlock. Of sorts."

I raised a brow. "Of sorts?"

"You ever see the Harry Potter movies?"

"Actually, no."

"Good. The woman who wrote it got it all wrong. Wizards aren't as powerful as the author... what's her name?"

"J.K. Rowling." I'd read the books, but he asked if I saw the movies, which I hadn't.

"Yeah, that's it. She's got wizards as the be-all and end-all, but they're not as powerful as warlocks. But when you combine the two, we're pretty effective."

"You're a mix?"

"Yes, ma'am."

"I hate it when you call me that."

"I know. You do this little thing with your lip." He smiled. "Makes me laugh."

I tapped my foot. "With all due respect, Chief, while you've got me locked in here giving me the history of the MBI, Austin Reynolds is out there trying to—what exactly is he trying to do?"

He pulled out a chair across from me, flipped it so the back faced me, and straddled it. "When your powers were unbound, you only gained a portion of them back. Once you put that charm on the chain with the star, the rest of them will return." He smiled. "And you will truly be the most powerful witch around."

"And let me guess, the MBI wants to take full advantage of that?"

He nodded.

Pigs would ride on brooms before I let that happen. And as for sweet Chief Gabe and me, I wasn't sure we had a future. Call me a hypocrite, but I lied to him because that was the rule. He lied to get me to work for his organization. Too bad. I wouldn't do it. I just couldn't let them know that until after I got that necklace and handled Austin. And I had a strong feeling I needed Gabe to help with that.

"Does Austin know you're a magical?"

"No."

"Is Ryland a shifter?"

He laughed. "What's your obsession with shifters?"

"It's a little scary watching two men who look like Bigfoot's second cousins squaring off."

"Ryland's a warlock like me. Austin's a shifter, but he believes if he gets both pieces of the necklace, he can shift into a warlock and stay that way."

"Is it true?"

"We don't have a definitive answer on that."

I furrowed my brow. "I'm sorry, did you just say you don't know?"

He nodded.

I threw my arms up in the air. "In my book the MBI is this major magical conglomeration of supreme beings, but obviously, that's just fiction."

"Magic doesn't give all the answers. You know that."

"It gets pretty darn close." I pretended to ignore the obvious fact that it hadn't told me a heck of a lot lately. "So, let me guess. While we're sitting here, Austin's what? In limbo?"

Cooper butted up against my leg and said, "That's how they explained it to me."

"And he can't do anything about that because he doesn't have any powers." I tapped my finger on the table. "So sending him looking for the fake car alarm punks was a lie too?"

"No. He's doing that. In limbo, as you've called it."

"Did you even have a wife?"

He flinched.

Oh, maybe he did. "I'm sorry."

He swallowed. "No, I deserved that. I haven't been honest with you, but you should understand. You're protecting Stella from the truth."

"Because I'm required to."

"As am I." He paused and pressed his lips together, then released a breath. "And yes, I did have a wife."

He was right, but that didn't stop me from pouting like a child. "Was she magical?"

"Abby, we'll get to that, but first we need to deal with what's happening." His sad eyes and slight pout hit me straight on the forgiveness bone.

He was right again. I was beginning to hate that about him. "So, what do we do?"

"We go back to the station, and you go back to the car. Set off my alarm again and—"

"You know I did that?"

"I know a lot of things."

"Right. Makes sense." I wondered what else he knew. "Then what?"

"We'll go back in time, and I'll send Austin out."

"But going back in time and changing things is dangerous. What about the people not involved? What happens to them?"

"We're strong together, and the MBI will make sure this is a solo incident. We can do that."

I wanted to believe him, but I just didn't know enough to feel comfortable with that answer. "Then what?"

"We'll have our guys keep a watch, but I'll need you to run. Let him chase you. We need him to come after you. He thinks you've got the charm, and if we—"

"I do have the charm."

"For now, yes, but we'll keep that safely locked up here. When he—"

I waved my hands in the air, my palms facing him. "Uh, no way. The charm goes where I put it, or I'm out."

He closed his eyes slowly, then opened them again. "Abby, we can protect you and the charm."

"The charm is mine, and so is the necklace. I don't need you to help me. I'm perfectly capable of doing this on my own." Maybe.

He tried to take my hand across the table, but I jerked it back and stuffed it under my thighs. The expression on his face wasn't anger. It was sadness.

I didn't care. "Gabe, Austin's coming after my powers, which, by the way, seems to be a popular thing lately. He's not coming after yours, and he's not coming after the MBI's." I jabbed myself in the chest. "He wants mine. I should be the one to take him down."

"You will. All we want to do is help."

"And tell me what to do."

His eyes hardened. "It's not like that."

Arguing would do nothing but postpone ending everything,

and I knew that, so I stopped but didn't acquiesce. I just kept my decision to move forward my way to myself. "Fine." I stood. "Let's do this."

He laid out the rest of their plan. I was supposed to run until I got to the Holiday Hills Cemetery, where they had a special cage to hold Austin. They would force him to shift, and when he did, they would strip him of that ability permanently. Once captured, they'd get the necklace. I was on board for all of it until that last part. The necklace was mine, and I'd destroy it before I let them have it.

~

I hit Gabe's car alarm with a magical nose rub and darted behind the cruiser. Cooper clung to my legs. I tried to kick him off, but I couldn't. "What're you doing?"

"Protecting you!"

"My calf is fine," I said, but didn't finish the rest of my sentence because Austin burst out of the department.

Did I imagine his sharp pointed teeth?

I popped up from behind the car, looked him in the eyes, and then sprinted off. Thirty seconds later I wanted to collapse on the ground and die. My heart was beating so hard my chest was pumping through my shirt. I thought I was having a heart attack or a lung attack or whatever happened to people who were totally out of shape and stupidly thought they could sprint a block without keeling over in breathless abdominal pain.

"Please," I screamed. "Don't let my chest explode!" It wasn't a spell or a prayer. I was begging.

I made it almost a mile, which was about three quarters of the way to the cemetery, before having to slow my pace. I gave myself no credit for my extended sprint because I knew only a miracle had gotten me that far that fast.

I eyed the cage next to my family's tomb. The irony of it wasn't lost on me.

Gabe told me the cage wouldn't be visible to Austin, and instructed me to run through it and stop on the other side. When he reached it, the door would close behind him, and he'd be locked in magically.

Except I'd tweaked the plan just a bit. I ran into the cage and stopped.

I knew MBI operatives were all around me. I couldn't see them, but I could feel them, and I felt their angst when I stopped inside the cage. It was a gamble, but I put the odds on the cage closing whether I was in it or not.

And if I was right, I'd need to work fast to do what I planned. And it had to work because I was out of options.

"Abby, no!" Gabe's panicked words echoed in my head.

Austin's hair grew so fast and thick even a tripled-edged razor wouldn't help. When he ran into the cage, the door locked behind him. He heard the click and whipped around. He must have seen the cage then because he gripped the metal bars and shook so hard I tumbled to the ground. I pushed myself back up, watching Cooper hiss from the other side of the bars.

Austin whipped around and narrowed his eyes at me, hissing. I jerked back, immediately regretting my decision to handle things on my own. He stepped closer to me and growled like a wolf. I took another step back and felt the cold metal of the cage pressing against my shirt. I shivered. I prayed. I rubbed under my nose and gave it my best shot.

The cage lifted in the air and swirled like a funnel, rising higher and higher. Gabe's yells faded away. As the cage rocked and spun, hairy, wolf-like, monster Austin lost his balance, knocked into the sides, and howled. As his body hit the hard metal, it morphed back to its human form. He was definitely a shifter.

Shifters could do some serious damage to witches, but I

wasn't the average witch, and from what I could tell, Austin's shifter button wasn't working right.

He tried to howl again, but it sounded more like a whine. I kicked him in the shin, and he went down like a bully on a playground. "That's for hurting Bessie." I kicked him again. "That's for acting like you liked me!" One more kick to the other shin. "Give me back my necklace!"

He fell to the metal floor. The cage crashed to the ground, sending me off balance and falling on top of him. His nails dug into my waist. I screamed and rolled off him, hitting the side of the cage.

I should have thought my plan through. I was able to see where we'd landed, which was close to where I'd hoped, but as I pushed myself up to stand, Austin pounced on top of me, sending the breath from my lungs in a heavy swoosh. I gasped for breath, felt the pain searing through my lungs each time I sucked in even a small amount of air. The pain was so intense, I couldn't think clearly. It took a second, but I regained my senses and rubbed under my nose. I landed outside the cage as planned, thanking God and the Universe for the help.

Cooper grabbed onto my leg and squeezed tight.

Austin pulled on the bars and stared at us. "I'll get that charm from you!"

I hit the bar with my palm, wincing as I breathed. "Good luck. I'm out here, and you're in there."

He pounded his fists on the metal bars as I dragged my finger under my nose. He wound up cuffed to the cage with a red-and-white bandana tied around his mouth.

I shook my finger at him. "That's what you get."

He narrowed his eyes at me.

Cooper swiped at my hip. "Uh, we're in the hall of our apartment building. Maybe you should move him inside?"

"That's the plan." It took a few rubs on my nose, but I finally got the cage squeezed into my small living area. It bumped against the back of my couch and blocked the entrance to my bedroom.

Austin gripped the bars and shook them, yelling words even Stella didn't use.

Cooper stared at him. "How'd the face thing come off?"

"Beats me." I'd calmed my heartbeat and could breathe better. It still hurt, but the pain was less intense than before.

"You'll give me the charm," Austin snarled.

"Yes, you're right. I will. When my cat here turns human." I looked down at Coop. "That would take a pretty major spell, though, don't you think? Probably going to need the necklace and charm to make that happen."

Cooper's small eyes popped open. "Uh, can we talk?"

I brushed him off.

"You think I'm the only one?" Austin's laugh had a bite to it. "You're pitiful.

I'm not the only one who wants that charm. I've got helpers."

I whipped my finger under my nose, and the bandana balled into a little bunch and stuck itself inside his mouth. The anger in his eyes sent me back two steps. Was I in over my head? Was someone else lying to me? Who else was a magical and hadn't told me? Stella?

No way. She was my best friend. She wouldn't hide something like that from me. Except I was hiding the very same thing from her, so who's to say she wouldn't do the same? I leaned toward the cage, and as Austin shook it again, I magically changed the location of the cuffs. Instead of being bound to each limb and attached to the cage bars, I bound them together, each hand to the opposite leg.

Cooper meowed. "Impressive."

My house shook. I lost my balance and leaned against the side of the couch to stay upright. It shook again, and I tumbled to the floor. I pulled myself back up through what felt like an earthquake. My abdomen hurt with each focused breath I took. I knew the feeling. When I was twelve I crashed my bike down a hill and broke three ribs. I couldn't breathe right for weeks.

I'd definitely broken a rib.

"What's going on?" Cooper asked.

"I think it's an earthquake." Though North Georgia wasn't susceptible to earthquakes and I'd never been in one, it sure felt like that's what was happening. Frames fell from my bookcase. My coffee table slid across the floor. The firewood next to my fireplace rolled off its stand. A picture of my mother, Mr. Charming, and Bessie fell from the wall, the glass frame shattering to pieces on the floor.

The front door burst open, and Gabe charged in with three men I'd never seen before. He tossed his hand in the air and waved it dismissively, and the cage and everything in it disappeared.

I pulled myself from the ground and barreled toward Gabe. "No!" I pushed his chest with my fists. "Bring him back, now!"

He held my shoulders. "Abby, calm down."

The other men searched my apartment, most likely looking for the charm.

I watched them open my dresser drawers and cringed. "Make them stop."

"We just want to protect you. To keep you safe."

He blocked my entrance to my bedroom, and I shoved him aside with a nose tap. "Get out! Now! I had him! I can get the necklace on my own!" The three men looked up at me but quickly went back to what they were doing. "I said get out!" I tapped my nose three times, and one by one the men disappeared.

Gabe held my shoulders from behind. "Abby, stop!"

I jerked free from his grasp. Cooper grabbed Gabe's pants leg between his teeth and yanked hard enough that Gabe fell to the ground. I stood over him, tapped my nose, and sent him someplace far enough away that I hoped he couldn't easily return. I swiped my hands together and pretended that didn't hurt my heart.

Cooper crawled onto the bed and stared at my messy apartment. "This happens to you a lot."

"Right?" I magically whipped it back into shape.

"Did you clean my litter?"

I narrowed my eyes at him.

"I'm just sayin'."

I collapsed onto the bed. "I need to find Austin."

He sauntered over and sat next to my hip. "Maybe we could use a little help."

"I don't know who to trust."

"Okay, okay." He walked around to my other hip and sat there. "I know I'm not the most trusting cat in town, but I gotta tell ya, I think Gabe's good people, and besides, he's got Austin. You don't have to find him. You just have to trust Gabe."

"He lied to me."

"Keeping something from you isn't a lie."

I disagreed. "It's called lying by omission." I rolled over and faced the window.

"Then Bessie lied, and I lied, and you've lied, and most importantly, your mother lied."

I wiped a tear from my eye. "Those are different."

"No, they're not, and I don't think you're mad at Gabe for not telling you the truth."

I rolled over and stared at my cat. "Then what am I mad about?"

"You wanted him to be human."

Cats are too intuitive, especially the magical ones. It's annoying as all get-out, too.

"Your life's changed a lot. You grew up thinking things were one way, but they're not. You wanted normal because it's what you know, and Gabe was part of that. Now all of a sudden, he's a magical, and he works for a magical superpower, and you don't like it."

"I don't."

"You don't get it, do you?"

"Get what?"

"Everything happens for a reason, Ab."

"What possible reason could be big enough to change my life so completely and take the one man I'd begun to trust and make him something else?"

"I don't know, but I do know acting like a spoiled brat isn't going to make any of this easier."

I narrowed my eyes at him.

"Hey, don't shoot the messenger, all right? It's my job to protect you, even if that means protecting you from yourself. Things have been tough. I get that. People aren't what they appear to be, but that's nothing new, and it's not the last time you'll see that, either. Should I mention names?"

I glared at him. "No. I get your point."

"Good, then brush it off and get over it. You've got a thing out there trying to hurt you and the people you love. So get off your bed, wipe your tears, forgive Gabe, and do what needs to be done."

He was right. I crawled off my bed and headed into my family room. I gently removed the family book from my shelf and set it on the coffee table.

Cooper stared at me.

"What?"

He stood up on his hind legs and rubbed his tummy with his paw.

"Oh for the love of magic." I shuffled to the kitchen and popped open a can of the good stuff, then set it on the counter.

"All that psychological babble makes a cat hungry." He num-nummed his way through the watery fish.

I returned to the book and flipped through the pages. There

had to be something in it to help me make sense of everything. As things in my life progressed, pages added to the book, pages relevant to my life. Sometimes those pages held spells, sometimes stories, but they usually made sense and helped me move forward.

The MBI wasn't fictional like I'd thought. Originally it was called the Mystical Bureau of Magicals, or MBM for short. The book didn't explain the name change, but I suspected it had something to do with the elimination of shifters and wizards. I had no clue why they were kicked out of the club, but I'd bet it was political. Everything was political, even in the magical world.

Witches and warlocks were the most powerful of all, and it was becoming more and more clear that they liked to push that power onto others. Including me. And I had to find a way to work with them, because as magical as I was, force was in numbers, and I couldn't fight them for long.

It was time I took my cat's advice and grew up.

CHAPTER 10

J fell asleep with the book on the coffee table and
Cooper in a tuna coma next to me on the couch. I'd
called Bessie before nodding off, and assured she was okay, I let
my body relax. I woke up with a start, sending Cooper flying off
my chest and onto the floor.

"Sorry about that. I didn't know you were there."

He glared at me.

"I said I'm sorry." I shuffled to the shower and got ready like it
was any other day. Mostly because I smelled and no magic in the
world could get rid of days-old sweaty smell. When I walked in
the back entrance of The Enchanted, it looked and felt different.
I knew it wasn't, but for me, things had changed once again.

Bessie poured me a cup of coffee. "You okay?"

I nodded. I hadn't told her everything I'd learned. I would
eventually, but I needed to find Austin and the necklace, and if
that meant working with Gabe and those magical men in black,
then so be it.

Mr. Charming flew over to me and picked at my bun. I gave
him a pat and leaned my head into him. I missed the bird, but I
had a feeling he'd found his new home with Bessie.

"Has Gabe been in?"

Bessie shook her head. "It's been quieter than usual." She went behind the counter and turned toward the pots of coffee brewing behind her.

I slid my finger under my nose and said a short protection spell. Just in case.

Three people walked into the store and stood in line behind me. I moved away and said goodbye to Mr. Charming as I walked out.

He flapped his wings in response.

Cooper rubbed up against my leg. "I kind of miss that squawker."

"Right there with you." I got in my car. "But I think he's chosen his person."

Cooper sighed. "I think you're right."

"When this is all over, I'll have a talk with Bessie. Make it official." A tear fell from my eye. "Nothing ever stays the same, does it?"

"Nope, and life is full of surprises. I never thought I'd be walking on all fours."

I stared at him. "Were you human before?"

He shook his head.

"A magical?"

"All familiars have a little magic in them."

"You know what I mean."

He nodded. "And like I said before, we'll talk about it another time." He stretched out and got comfy in my passenger seat. "Where are we going?"

"To the MBI."

"Alrighty then. Let's do this."

I drove to the MBI headquarters, but the two-story window-less building wasn't there. "I don't understand."

"I was afraid this would happen." Cooper propped his front paws on the passenger window. "It's mobile."

"The building?"

He nodded as he stared outside. "Magic is everywhere, so the headquarters goes where it's needed."

"But I need it."

He faced me. "It's not always about you."

"I'm not saying it is, but come on, they're trying to recruit me. You'd think they'd stay visible for me."

"Try the PD. He's still got a real job, you know."

I nose-rubbed us to the station. No point in wasting time.

"Is the chief in?"

The front desk officer smiled. "He's waiting for you."

I stared at Cooper.

He blinked. "Guy knows you pretty well."

I rolled my eyes. Gabe knew my familiar pretty well because he was the one who suggested we try the station.

She escorted us into his office, and Gabe popped up from his chair. "I'm sorry about last night."

I held up my hand. "I'm here to work with you, pretty much under duress, so let's get this over with, okay?"

He nodded once and sat down. "We're on your side."

"Where's Austin?"

"He's at the MBI, locked up in a safe place."

"Where'd you put the MBI? I went there, but it's gone."

The corner of his mouth twitched. "It's there. You just didn't look hard enough." He grabbed his keys from the desk drawer. "Let's go."

Cooper and I followed him out the back entrance to where he'd parked his cruiser. "I need to know everything."

"And you will, I promise."

"The necklace is mine."

"I know that."

"And I'm not giving you or anyone else the charm."

"I know that too."

"And I don't know if things will ever be the same between us."

"I don't expect they will." He turned toward me as he left the parking lot. "They'll be better."

"I'm glad one of us thinks that."

He backed his car out of the department's lot. "Abby, I know this is a lot to take in, but if you step back and look at it all through my eyes, you'll understand my motivation."

"Drive slow."

He whipped his head in my direction. "What?"

"I need to know about your wife."

He breathed in deeply, then released the air slowly. "What do you want to know?"

"Was she human or magical?"

He closed his eyes for a moment, then opened them and said, "She was human."

"Oh." I wasn't expecting that answer. "What happened to her?"

"She was diagnosed with cancer, stage one, but they were wrong. She was gone six weeks after we got the news."

A lump appeared in the middle of my throat. I swallowed hard to push it down. "I'm sorry."

"She was thirty. Too young to die."

I wondered if he could have done something, but I knew the answer. Witches and warlocks only had so much power, and we couldn't stop what was meant to be.

"She wanted children, but I wanted to wait. I was worried what would happen because I'm a…" He left the end of that sentence unsaid.

"I understand."

"I never thought I could feel the way I felt about her again. Then I met you."

What was he trying to say?

He pulled the car over to the side of the road and put it in park, then shifted his position to face me. "I never meant to hurt you. I couldn't keep my wife safe, but I can keep you safe, and I promise I won't let you down. I don't want to lose what we have."

I bit my lip. "I don't either."

He smiled. "Good. Then let's go kick some shifter butt. Together."

I smiled. "Yes, sir."

He put the car back in drive. "Don't call me that. It's almost as bad as Miss Odell and ma'am."

"Nothing is as bad as ma'am."

He laughed.

We pulled into the MBI's blacktop parking lot. I'm always fascinated when Georgia companies, magical or not, use blacktop. The stuff melts easily in high temperatures, and Georgia can get close to one hundred degrees in the spring. When blacktop melts, it sticks to tires, shoes, cat feet, everything. I guess a major magical corporation wouldn't care about that, but I did. I invest a lot in my shoes, and I didn't want to waste the money because someone was too cheap to make a better parking lot.

Gabe escorted Cooper and me into a large conference room, where he told us to wait and they'd be in shortly. He offered me a coffee and Cooper a bowl of milk. Cooper took the milk, but I didn't accept the coffee. I had no appetite, and no desire for anything to drink unless it was one of Bessie's magical drinks.

Cooper was in awe, staring at the large leather couch, ten-seater oak table, and cushioned leather chairs on wheels. He sat in one of the chairs and I spun him around while we waited. "Whoa. I'm getting dizzy."

I rolled my eyes. "Then stop spinning."

"I'm still spinning from all that mushy talk I had to suffer through in the car."

"I feel awful for being mad at him."

"You should."

"Whose side are you on?"

"I'm a cat. I'm on my side."

"One of these days you're going to tell me the truth."

"You can't handle the truth."

"That's another movie line, isn't it?"

"Wow. Look at you, getting your movie trivia on."

"It was on Netflix. Gabe and I watched it a few weeks ago. He repeated the line, like, five times before the movie ended."

"I was there, remember?"

"We're going to have to send you to Bessie's when I have dates."

"Probably smart. No one needs to see that level of awkwardness happening."

"You're such a snot."

"But I'm cute."

"If you say so."

Gabe returned with the three men in black suits. They all sat on one side of the table.

I shifted in my seat, which suddenly didn't feel all that comfortable. "Why does it feel like I'm going to be interrogated?"

Gabe smiled, but the other men's faces stayed stoic and annoying. He leaned forward, his gentle eyes easing my discomfort. "Abby, we have some bad news."

My heart dropped. "Bessie? Stella? What's wrong?"

"No, they're okay. It's the necklace. Austin doesn't have it, and we can't find it."

I raised an eyebrow. "You can't find it?" I pointed at each of them individually. "You're like characters from a graphic novel, but real, and you can't find a simple necklace?"

"It's more complicated than that," he said.

I nodded. "Em hmm."

"Since the necklace is rightfully yours, we think it's being hidden from all of us and that you're the only one who can find it."

"But Austin's a shifter. He can't cast spells."

"I know."

"So that means someone's helping him." I smacked my hand on the table. "He told me that. He's working with someone."

"That's what we're beginning to think too."

"So what am I supposed to do?" I rubbed under my nose and asked for the necklace to appear. It didn't. "It won't come to me. Do you have a crystal pendulum? I'm pretty good with those now."

He shook his head. "We tend to stay with the traditional magical components."

"What does that mean?"

"You know, spices, potions, wands, those kinds of things."

"Hold on." I imagined my crystal and iPad, then rubbed under my nose. They appeared on the table in front of me. "Let's get this over with." I tried to locate the necklace, but whoever cast a hiding spell over it was powerful.

"What about Austin? Try locating him."

The pendulum zoomed in on a large open space on the outskirts of town. "Is this where we are?"

Gabe nodded. "I think you're right. Austin's working with someone. We'll figure out who, and we'll find the necklace."

"What about me? I want to help."

"No, it's not safe."

"I'm a witch. I can get myself out of dangerous situations." I wasn't too sure that was true, but I wanted to stay positive.

"I know that, but we need you here so we can connect the necklace and the charm."

"Can I ask you something?"

He nodded once.

"What's in it for the MBI? It's my necklace, so why all the effort?"

"You're an asset, Abby. We need you on our team."

"But that's a decision I make, not you."

"Of course."

"So if you want me on board, I need to be involved."

Cooper climbed off his chair and rubbed up against my leg.

Gabe furrowed his brow. "Abby."

"Sir."

He got the message. "Fine. You can go with us, but you have to follow our lead."

Cooper rubbed up against me again. What was he trying to do, send messages through my skin?

"Fine, but I need a guarantee that the necklace and charm will stay with me, and any decision to come on board with your magical men in black team is my choice."

"I promise."

I paced the conference room. "So, basically, I'm a decoy."

Gabe cringed. "I'm sure there's a better word for it."

I tapped my finger on my chin. "Not that I can think of, and words are my jam."

He smirked. "But you're on board?"

"Yes."

He smiled.

I rubbed under my nose, and a small box appeared on the table. When I sneezed and it disappeared, I held up my hands. "Sorry, my bad."

The corner of his mouth twitched.

Another rub, and the box reappeared. "Let's do this."

Gabe squeezed my shoulder. Cooper rubbed against my leg.

"Ryland is on his way. He and I will be in the shadows, and we'll keep you safe, Abby."

"What about Stella?"

The conference room door swung open, and Ryland entered.

My body stiffened. "Where's Stella?"

"She's safe. Don't worry."

"I am worried. Where is she?"

He flung his arm and a live feed appeared on the flat-screen TV on the wall. I watched Stella sip a cup of coffee at The Enchanted. Bessie was behind the counter, and Mr. Charming perched on the chair across from my best friend.

"They're at The Enchanted. How is that safe?"

"It's not the real Enchanted. It's a mirror image, but in a safe place. Austin can't get to them."

I bit my bottom lip. "Does Bessie know what's happening?"

He nodded. "She knows we're protecting her, but Stella's life isn't different. Not at this point." His eyes softened. "I won't let anyone hurt her or Bessie. I promise."

The plan was to let Austin loose and hope he'd lead us to the necklace. I'd serve as his motivation.

The idea was for me to appear angry and betrayed, which would push Austin to think I let my guard down, was weak, maybe even defenseless—all far from the truth—and get him to come to me. Once he did, we'd trap him and get the necklace.

We magically transported my car to the MBI and set the plan in motion. I drove toward home, stopping first at Bessie's house to place a protection spell over it just in case. I then went to Stella's and did the same. I drove to the remains of my mother's home, placed a small black box where the other used to be hidden, and said a quick revealing spell that would allow anyone with a pendulum to locate me and the box. It sounded silly, but even magicals took the easy route, so if Austin's partner tried, he or she could find the box and think it was the charm. If that happened, five MBI warlocks were waiting in the wings.

I didn't expect Austin to fall for that, though. He was smart, and he'd go where I went. He'd send his minion partner to the box so he could take care of the witch.

I went home and waited. I heard additional MBI guys outside. They weren't being inconspicuous, but maybe they weren't trying. I dusted my bookshelves, emptied and loaded the dishwasher, and rearranged my sock drawer. Who knew I had so many socks? I tossed six pairs, then regretted that and stuffed them back into the small drawer. I changed my sheets, then washed the ones I'd removed, dried them, and ironed them. I've never ironed my sheets before, and after doing that, knew I'd never do it again.

Finally, I got the call. Austin was out, and they'd tracked him to my mother's old house. I was surprised he went there. I thought for sure he'd come for me. Maybe his partner sent him for the package instead?

Cooper had been snoozing on the back of the couch. I poked him in the side. "You ready?"

He stretched. "Can I get a can of tuna before we go?"

I rolled my eyes. "You should have eaten when I put out the last can."

"I needed a nap."

I scooped him up and carried him over my forearm with his feet dangling.

"Cats really don't like being carried this way."

"Can I trust you to not dart to the kitchen?"

"My first job is to keep you safe. My second is to eat. Or sleep. It depends on my activity level."

He got another eye roll, but I set him down, and he followed me to my car and climbed onto my passenger seat. "You ready for this?"

"Don't really have another choice, do I?"

"Why are we driving instead of just showing up there?"

"I want to keep things as normal as possible."

"Right. Let me know how that works out."

I parked down the street from the house. My senses went into overdrive, and I heard everything around me. Every bird chirp, every leaf crunch, every tire roll down the side streets. I spotted three men in black suits and dark shades on the other side of the street. They nodded when I looked at them.

Cooper walked in front of me, and I nearly tripped over him. "Inconspicuous, aren't they?"

I shrugged. "I don't think they're trying to be."

We stood in the front yard of my mother's home. I examined the burned-out frame, wishing with all my might I could restore it. Magic could do it, but the humans would still see it as the destroyed remains of my mom's life. I empathized with the people who'd purchased the house, but I never really felt it was theirs. I doubted most people in town saw it as theirs either. My mother was very popular, and people always talked about her. She was missed, and that house helped others feel like she was still around. It was heartbreaking that it was gone. My thoughts were interrupted by a soft, low growl. I trembled. Here we go.

Austin's shifter form stepped out from behind the trees on the right side of the home. He didn't charge toward me, and he didn't poof out his chest like angry shifters did in the movies. He just stood there, growling and watching me.

I stared back and stepped closer.

He growled again.

I took another step toward him, my hands shaking and my knees weak. "You're a lot more attractive without the full body fur. Why don't you drop the act? You know you can't beat me."

He charged toward me. Cooper hissed. I pushed my hands in front of me, and Austin flew backward. He regained his balance and came at me faster, but I kept pushing him back, hitting him harder each time.

Austin growled loudly, then shifted from side to side before running toward the side of the house where I'd buried the empty box. I ran after him, sucking in large gulps of air to fill my lungs. Cooper raced in front of me, reaching the box before either of us.

Four legs are always faster than two.

He stood with it underneath his body and hissed at Austin,

who swung his clawed paw at my familiar and sent him flipping through the air.

I screamed and charged Austin without any regard for my own safety. "No one messes with my familiar!" I screamed, pushing until I flung Austin into the burned-out parlor. He fell to the ground and pounced back up. I pushed him again, sending all of my power through my veins and out my fingertips.

I wasn't surprised at my growing abilities. I was grateful. The powers that be were shining down on me, and I knew I could stop him.

Cooper ran over, and as Austin climbed off the burned chair, my cat jumped on top of his face and covered his eyes. Austin grabbed him and tossed him aside. I screamed again. I was losing control, but it wasn't supposed to go like this. I had to get the charm back or Gabe would take over, and I couldn't let that happen. I needed to be the one to stop him.

"You want the charm? It's not in the box."

Austin's head tilted, and he grunted.

I pulled the small silver piece from my pocket and held it up. "Let's negotiate a deal."

He was so fast I barely saw him coming. One minute I was dangling the charm like a carrot, and the next I was on the ground like a quarterback in the Super Bowl. I went down with a thud, my head smacking the hard Georgia clay. I was dizzy and discombobulated. Something heavy trapped me on the ground. It smelled like expired uncooked hamburger meat.

I pushed at Austin, but he was stronger than me. "Get off me!" When he wouldn't move, I pushed again magically and rolled to my side as he went flying into the air. He landed a few feet away on the boulder my mom had shipped from Amicalola Falls. The thing was the size of a Volkswagen Bug. When he hit the boulder, it must have knocked him out, because he didn't move.

When Austin's body transformed back to its human version, I knew the blow was fatal, but I wasn't sure how I felt about it.

Gabe and Ryland appeared beside Austin's remains. I fell to my knees to catch my breath and gather my senses. Tears fell from my eyes, splashing onto the ground. Cooper rubbed against me. I was so glad he was okay, I pulled him into my arms and cradled him against my head as he purred.

"I'm so sorry," I whispered.

"It was nothing. I was a distraction. That was my plan."

I didn't believe him, but I didn't care. I was just glad he was okay, and that it was all over.

Only it wasn't. I set my familiar back on the ground. "We don't know who was helping him. We need to find out and stop them or this won't end well."

A loud bang shook the ground. Cooper pounced and ran toward the rock. I stood frozen at the sight before me.

Three cages similar to the ones I'd created circled the sides and back of the rock. Gabe, Bessie, and Stella were each in one, their hands and feet cuffed to the sides. Their mouths were covered, and all but Stella's eyes were blocked, too.

Austin's human form had reappeared, and he stood next to Ryland. They both smirked at me.

I pointed to Ryland. "You?"

Gabe shook his cage. Where were the other men in black suits? What had Ryland done to them?

"Give us the charm, and we'll let your friends go," Ryland said.

Cooper moved forward.

"Cooper, no, please."

He stopped and stared at me.

"It's okay," I whispered.

Ryland stepped closer. "We're done playing around, Abby. Give us the charm."

I rubbed my righthand pocket, feeling the small piece secured at the bottom. "Come and get it."

Gabe's cage rocked. I heard him trying to talk, but I couldn't make out what he was saying through the cloth stuffed in his mouth.

Ryland moved like a character in a science fiction movie. One second he was beside the rock, and the next, right in front of me. As I stepped back, he stepped closer, and as he swung his arm, I blocked it with my forearm, then jerked to the side. He came at me again, and I knocked him away.

Using my mind to generate my magic came easily.

He fell backward, then steadied himself and swung at me again. His powers hit me and I fell, but I got back up and swung toward him. He fell, then Austin morphed back into his furry ugly self. I flung him to the side, imagining him as a toad, and ignored his growl as it deepened into a low croak.

Ryland wasn't impressed. He waved his hand and Austin appeared next to him again. "You can't win. Hand over the charm, and you won't have to watch your friends die."

"You wouldn't dare!"

Ryland smiled. "Try me."

I dug my hand into my pocket and cupped the small charm in my palm. I held it to my heart and prayed I was doing the right thing. Gabe shook his cage again. I stared at Bessie. She couldn't see either, but like Gabe, she knew what was happening. Magicals sensed things. Her chin dropped. They thought I was giving in, destroying myself and probably them too, but I wasn't.

I was saving them.

I brought my fist to my mouth and kissed it. As I stretched out my arm and opened my palm, I whispered, "Return what is mine and vanish the thieves for all time."

The necklace appeared in my hand. I closed my fingers around the necklace and charm, watching as tiny sparkles of light drifted out from my fingers. Austin and Ryland both screamed. I watched as they disintegrated into small dark blobs before sinking into the ground. I opened my palm, and the charm—now attached to the necklace—and the star lit up. The cages disappeared, and Gabe and Bessie stood where they'd been. But Stella was gone.

My heart raced. "Where's Stella?"

Bessie walked over to me. "It's okay." She wrapped me in a hug I needed more than air. "She's where she belongs, and she won't remember any of this." She tried to release me, but I held on tighter. "You did it, Abby. You did it!"

Gabe smiled as I loosened my grip on Bessie. I wasn't sure what to think, and I definitely didn't know what to say. But when he pulled me into his arms, none of that mattered. I knew I was where I belonged.

CHAPTER 11

*E*smerelda *closed the door to her new office. She admired the white walls, clean glass desk, and framed photos on the wall. This is good, she thought. I could get used to this.*

A knock disrupted her pleasant feeling.

"It's open."

Her new boss, Aberdeen Wilder, stepped in. "Esmerelda, we have an assignment for you. We need you in London this evening."

And just like that, her new life began.

Mr. Charming perched on my shoulder. He picked at a few loose strands of hair and made little chirping sounds that were music to my ears. Doc Hetty opened The Enchanted's door and smiled at me. He waited at the counter while Bessie poured him a fresh cup of coffee. "How's the story going?"

"It's good, thanks for asking. You have a busy day ahead?"

"Sure do. We're seeing six new patients today. If this keeps up, I may need to get myself a partner."

"That's exciting."

He patted my shoulder. "Got you to thank for that."

"Don't thank me. I just did what had to be done."

"That's one way to look at it." He took a sip of his coffee. "Best be getting to the office now. You take care, you hear?"

"You too, Doc."

Bessie sat down across from me. "What a nice man. He will be forever grateful to you."

"I didn't do anything."

"Abigail Odell, that's ridiculous. You saved his practice. Getting rid of the threat like you did and reversing the damage? I haven't seen a witch tackle something that big since—"

"Since my mom?"

She smiled. "You're just like her, you know. Even more so now that you've come into your true powers."

Things had changed, but I was getting used to things changing. "I've decided I'm not taking the job."

Her eyes widened. "With the MBI? Why not?"

"I want to write about witches saving their towns and the people they love, not be that witch. It's not who I am."

"But it's your calling."

"No, it's not. My calling is doing what I'm doing. I know this now." I touched the charm and star on the necklace. "This wasn't about me being some magical superpower. This was about me finding myself." I pushed my laptop to the side. "Remember when I was trying to figure out things with Gabe?"

She nodded.

"You said all I had to do was look within myself and I'd find the answers. And when you were in that cage, that's what I did. I'd tried to retrieve the necklace before, but I couldn't. I didn't trust myself enough. I wasn't ready, but then, seeing the three people I cared about the most caged like wild animals, knowing you could all die? My need to save you gave me strength, it gave me power. Not the charm in my hand. Wanting to help you showed me what I needed to see, told me what to do. The spell to eliminate Ryland and Austin wasn't something I'd thought up and planned. It just happened."

"That's how magic is supposed to work."

"Yes, but I didn't really get that. I mean, I've been learning the tricks and stuff, and I've figured out a thing or two, but I didn't *get it*." I sipped my hot tea. "Now I do, and I know I'm not supposed to work for some magical organization. Let them do their thing, and I'll do mine."

"And what is that?"

"Making people happy with my writing and keeping the people I love safe."

She smiled.

"I've made a decision, Bessie. This is my last book as a ghostwriter. The next one will be under my name."

"You're going to write Esmerelda under your own name?"

I shook my head. "No, I can't. But I can create a new character, and I already have." I slid my laptop around and showed her the title page of my new manuscript.

She read it out loud. *"Let's Hear it for the Witch: An Adelle Arden Paranormal Cozy Mystery* by Abigail Odell." Her eyes widened. "Oh, Abby, I'm so happy for you!"

I smiled. "Me, too! Going out on my own is scary, but I've already talked to the publisher, and as long as Adelle isn't too similar to Esmerelda, and if all the boxes are checked, they'll publish her story."

"What about the diva author and Esmerelda? How's that going to work?"

"Esmerelda's new job will take her in a different direction, and the publisher's already looking for another ghostwriter. I haven't talked to the diva author. She called, but I didn't answer."

"And you're not going to call her back, are you?"

"I finished the last book, and it's in the editing process. If they want changes, I'll make them, but I'm done with that woman."

"Speaking of being done with people."

I sighed. It had been a month since I sent Austin and Ryland away. At first, things with Gabe were a little shaky, but in the past week, that changed. I wasn't angry at him for keeping a secret. I had no right to be. But I was worried that my decision not to work with the MBI would somehow separate us. He'd come to Holiday Hills for me, and I was no longer an option for the MBI. What if they transferred him?

When I asked him that, he smiled and said, "I'm a cop, and I have a job here in Holiday Hills. I'm not going anywhere."

From that moment on, things with Gabe made sense. We were in it for the long haul, and I knew we'd make it.

I'd been able to reverse the bad things Austin and Ryland had done. Doc's office was intact, and the family who lived in my mom's house never knew anything had happened.

There hadn't been any more fires. There hadn't been any Ryland. Stella was still single, and the available men in Holiday Hills still forced her to review her options on dating apps. Which meant I'd be doing a lot of magical checking on everyone she dated. Ryland used her, and even though she couldn't remember him, I could, and I wasn't going to let someone do that again.

My thoughts traveled back to Gabe, to his soft smile, his loving eyes. Everything about him seemed magical in that way new love always felt.

As if he knew I was thinking about him, he walked into The Enchanted. When our eyes met, a smile stretched across my face.

Bessie hopped out of her seat and scooted behind the counter. "Well hey, Chief. It's so nice to see you! You want the usual this morning?"

"That'd be great, Bessie, thank you."

I glanced at him and caught him staring at me. He smiled and walked over.

"Hey."

"Hey," I said back. "Did they agree?"

He smiled. "It's a go."

I quietly clapped my hands. "Can we tell her?"

"That's your job."

Mr. Charming had flown toward the back of the store earlier, but when he heard Gabe's voice, he made his presence known. Cooper disappeared into the back of the store.

Gabe flicked his head toward my laptop. "How's the book coming?"

"Oh, it's great."

"I'm sure it'll be a best seller."

"Maybe."

Bessie handed him his coffee. Mr. Charming settled himself on her shoulder and picked at her head.

"Bess, we have some news."

Her jaw dropped. "You're getting married, aren't you? I knew it!"

My eyes widened. "No, uh, that's not it." I glanced at Gabe. The look of shock on his face made me laugh. "It's about Mr. Charming."

Her jaw tensed. "Is he leaving us?"

"He's leaving me, not you."

"I…what?"

"Gabe knows some higher-ups, and he's secured Mr. Charming as your familiar."

"But I already have one."

I blanched. "You do?"

Gabe coughed. "The higher-ups think it's time to retire your other one and stick with the bird."

"Wait." I shook my head. "What's the other one?"

Cooper returned with a mouse hanging from his mouth.

I jumped from my seat and backed away from the table. "Cooper! Put it down!"

He dropped the mouse, who crawled onto Bessie's foot and up to her other shoulder. She smiled at him and patted his little head. "Hey, sweetie pie. Looks like you're going into retirement."

"Your familiar is a mouse?"

"Was a mouse," Cooper said. "Now it's the bird, and the mouse is prey."

I glared at him.

He sat up with his front paws in the air. "Kidding." He dropped his paws. "Chill out, Abs."

"Harry's been with me for as long as Mr. Charming was with your mom. They've both watched over us, but Harry's getting on in years, and mice don't live as long as parrots. The change will be good."

I was speechless. That didn't happen often.

Stella stormed in. "You will not believe the dream I had!" She caught the awkward look on my face and softened her stomping. "Oh, hey, Gabe. How're you?"

"Good, you?"

She pulled out a chair and sat at my table. "Bessie, I need a double shot, please. I was up all night after that dream!"

I leaned toward her. "What dream?"

"It was the weirdest thing."

Gabe turned toward the counter.

"Nope." Stella grabbed his wrist. "You gotta hear this. You were in it too."

Bessie walked to the espresso machine and prepared Stella's drink.

"We were outside of your mom's house. At least I think it was your mom's. It was burned to a crisp." She pointed to Bessie and then Gabe. "The three of us were in these weird cages."

I glanced at Gabe.

"Thank God that was just a dream," Bessie said. "I would have a heart attack if I was caged like that."

"I woke up so confused. It felt so real."

Bessie patted her on the shoulder. "Don't worry, honey, it was just a dream."

"I know that, but it was so strange. When I woke up, I was

wearing the same thing that I was in the dream. How does that even happen?"

I knew how, but I wasn't going to tell her the truth. "Maybe you sleep-dressed?"

She rolled her eyes. "Yeah, and you can time travel. Please."

Maybe I was wrong about Stella after all?

Who's That Witch?:
Holiday Hills Witch Cozy Mystery #3

Another witch has come to Holiday Hills... and a sudden string of strange events follows close behind.

Coincidence?

Abby doesn't think so. And she makes it her mission to get to the bottom of the mystery!

Get your copy today at
CarolynRidderAspenson.com

KEEP IN TOUCH WITH CAROLYN

Never miss a new release! Sign up to receive exclusive updates from Carolyn.

Join today at CarolynRidderAspenson.com

As a thank you for signing up, you'll receive a free novella!

The Holiday Hills Witch Cozy Mystery Series

There's a New Witch in Town

Witch This Way

Who's That Witch?

The Magical Real Estate Mystery Series

Spooks for Sale

Selling Spells Trouble

Cloaked Commission

The Angela Panther Mystery Series

Unfinished Business

Unbreakable Bonds

Uncharted Territory

Unexpected Outcomes

Unbinding Love

The Christmas Elf

The Ghosts

Undetermined Events

The Event

The Favor

Other Books

Mourning Crisis (The Funeral Fakers Series)

Join Carolyn's Newsletter List at

CarolynRidderAspenson.com

You'll receive a free novella as a thank you!

ACKNOWLEDGMENTS

This book wouldn't be what it is without the help and expertise of Severn River Publishing. Special thanks to Amber, the glue of SRP, and Cara, my editor, who made my story read so much better than I ever could.

A big shout out to Lynn Shaw, my PA, who's been with me from the start. You're a fantastic cheerleader and a good friend.

And most of all, thanks to my readers. To say I'm appreciative of your support is an understatement.

ABOUT CAROLYN

Carolyn Ridder Aspenson writes sassy, southern cozy mysteries featuring imperfect women with a flair for telling it like it is. Her stories focus on relationships, whether they're between friends, family members, couples, townspeople, or strangers, because ultimately, it's relationships that make a story.

Now an empty-nester, Carolyn lives in the Atlanta suburbs with her husband, two Pit Bull-Boxer mix dogs and two cantankerous cats, but you'll often find her at a local coffee shop people-watching (and listening.) Or as she likes to call it: plotting her next novel.

Join Carolyn's mailing list at
CarolynRidderAspenson.com

9 781648 750151